PASSING AS A FIREFLY

"All right," said Lennox. "Tell me what's involved in the process."

"As you wish, Mister Lennox," the surgeon said, exhaling deeply. "First, we will have to remove your arms and legs. The musculature and joints are all wrong. They will be replaced by prosthetic limbs that are identical to those of a Firefly. We will also shorten your torso and redesign your hip joints. The greatest amount of surgery will be on your face, since it will exposed at all times. We'll have to reshape the cheekbones and the jaw, eliminate the nose completely, give you eyes the same color as a Firefly's, elongate the skull, and eliminate all facial hair."

Lennox frowned. "How much of *me* will be left?"

"The essential you—your brain, your central nervous system, and your heart—will remain unchanged. We're not sure about your internal organs yet. You'll keep them, of course, but we may have to add a few . . ."

TOR BOOKS BY MIKE RESNICK

TOR BOOKS EDITED BY MIKE RESNICK

A MIRACLE
OF RARE DESIGN

A TRAGEDY OF TRANSCENDENCE

❂❂❂❂❂❂❂❂❂❂❂❂

Mike Resnick

A TOM DOHERTY ASSOCIATES BOOK
NEW YORK

This is a work of fiction. All the characters and events portrayed in this book are fictitious, and any resemblance to real people or events is purely coincidental.

A MIRACLE OF RARE DESIGN:
A TRAGEDY OF TRANSCENDENCE

Cover art by John Berkey

A Tor Book
Published by Tom Doherty Associates, Inc.
175 Fifth Avenue
New York, NY 10010

Tor Books on the World-Wide Web:
http://www.tor.com

Tor® is a registered trademark of Tom Doherty Associates, Inc.

ISBN: 0-812-52424-1
Library of Congress Card Catalog Number: 94-31317

First edition: December 1994
First mass market edition: February 1996

Printed in the United States of America

0 9 8 7 6 5 4 3 2 1

To Carol, as always,

And to the lovely ladies of GEnie

Pat Cadigan	Beth Meacham
Susan Casper	Lyn Nichols
Kate Daniel	Louise Rowder
Barbara Delaplace	Kristine Kathryn Rusch
Linda Dunn	Michelle Sagara
Mary Frey	Josepha Sherman
Esther Friesner	Susan Shwartz
Adrienne Gormley	Janna Silverstein
Lea Hernandez	Janni Simner
Nina Kiriki Hoffman	Martha Soukup
Kij Johnson	Judith Tarr
Katharine Kerr	Karen Taylor
Terry McGarry	Jane Yolen
Maureen F. McHugh	Leah Zeldes

Each and every one a rare miracle

ONE

Xavier William Lennox shuffled down the narrow, twisting street, trying to mimic the awkward walk of the Fireflies. He breathed in the pungent odors of decaying food, felt a slight burning sensation in his nostrils, and tried to ignore it.

He checked the sky. The huge yellow sun wouldn't set for another two hours, even though a trio of moons were already dancing above the horizon. That meant he'd have to stay here for at least another hour before making his final approach to the pyramid.

He looked around. Three Fireflies were standing outside the triangular doorway of a mud building, lost in conversation. They were wrapped in colorful robes, totally oblivious to the heat that was sapping Lennox's strength by the minute. He tried to hear what they were saying, but he was too far away, and he didn't dare move any closer: the last thing he needed was for some overly friendly Firefly to ask him to join them.

A Firefly infant, no more than two years old, toddled up to him, totally nude, his golden skin reflecting the sunlight, his tiny vestigial wings flapping furiously to no good purpose. Lennox looked away from the child, hoping that it would lose interest in him and wander off.

Suddenly it tugged at his robe.

"*Bebu?*" it asked. "*Bebu?*"

"I'm not your *bebu,*" replied Lennox, grateful that a toddler wouldn't be able to spot his accent as the alien words rolled uncomfortably off his tongue. "Go home."

"*Bebu?*" repeated the child.

Lennox looked around to make sure no one was watching him, then slowly lifted his arms and dropped them. It was a sign of aggression in the fierce, carnivorous avians, now almost extinct, that for eons had preyed upon the Fireflies. The infant instinctively recoiled at the gesture, then raced into an angular mud house. It would be, Lennox knew, a typical Firefly dwelling with no windows, crazy angles, and a high ceiling covered with their incomprehensible religious symbols.

A moment later the infant's mother stuck her head out of the doorway, looking at Lennox as the child pointed in his direction. After glaring at him for what she considered a sufficient length of time, she disappeared back inside the house, and Lennox released his grip on the pistol he had hidden beneath his flowing robes.

A bead of sweat trickled down his face, ran along his upper lip, and made its way into his mouth. Then another, and another, and suddenly he realized that he was thirsty. More than thirsty; he was in serious danger of dehydration. The thought infuriated him. He had spent so long training his body for this day that he felt betrayed by it. For reasons he could not comprehend, for all oxygen-breathers needed water and Medina was a sweltering hellhole, the Fireflies drank—sipped, really—only at sunrise and sunset. Now he would have to risk exposure by giving his body the water it craved while the sun was still high in the sky.

He slowly shuffled down the street, peering casually into the interior of each building he passed. Every one of them was occupied, and the thought of having to wait for water made him lust for it even more.

Finally he reached the end of the street and found himself confronted by five more crazily winding thoroughfares, all narrow, all crowded with angular buildings that made little or no sense. He bore to the right, not out of any belief that he was more likely to find an empty domicile there, but simply so he could find his way back, and again began inspecting each structure as he walked by. Fireflies of both sexes and all sizes stared out at him, neither speaking nor showing any interest.

Maybe it's even hot for *them,* he thought as he continued. About halfway down the street he came to a stable—the least likely place to put it, so of course that's where it was located—and stepped inside, grateful to be out of the sun despite the alien smells. There were ten stalls—seven on the left, three on the right, all irregularly shaped—and he walked slowly down the aisle between them, half-expecting to be stopped with every step he took.

But nobody was there to stop him, and he found that two of the stalls were empty. Trying to ignore the soft bleats of the shaggy, incredibly ugly beasts of burden—''They make old Earth's wildebeest look like creatures of grace and beauty,'' Fallico had remarked during their first visit to Medina—he entered a stall, sat in a corner below eye level of anyone passing by, quickly removed his canteen, and greedily poured half of it down his throat before pausing for breath.

He sat still for a moment, reveling in the relief from sun and thirst, then drained the canteen and walked over to the stall's water trough to refill it. The trough was empty.

He walked cautiously into the aisle and inspected all the other troughs. Evidently the beasts kept to the same schedule as their masters; there wasn't a drop of water to be had.

Lennox returned to the empty stall, buried the canteen beneath the bedding, and walked back out the way he had come. As he was about to leave the stable, he saw a pair of Fireflies approaching him. His first inclination was to duck back inside, but he quickly decided that was more likely to draw attention than simply walking down the street, swathed in his robes, acting as if he belonged there. His mind made up, he began walking directly toward the Fireflies, staring at the ground, circling around them without missing a step. They passed by silently, without giving him a second glance.

He smelled the odors of alien cooking. Good. The Fireflies were preparing for the evening meal. That meant the sun had to set pretty soon. The temperature would drop forty degrees or more in the next hour, and he could finally stop worrying about passing out from heat stroke.

Suddenly he became aware of a damp feeling in his armpits. *Damn!* Despite all his precautions, his salt pills, his adrenaline injections, the oxygenation of his blood, his antiperspirants, his loosely fitting robes, he had begun sweating in earnest. Perspiration was pouring off his body. How much longer before the stains were visible? More to the point, did Fireflies ever sweat? There was so much he didn't know about them; who would ever have thought that he might get tripped up by something so trivial as perspiration?

He stepped into a recessed doorway while he considered his options, and finally concluded that he didn't really have any. He hadn't come this far to quit, and he had no way of masking any stains if they should come through, so he might as well not worry about them. If he held his body awkwardly, if he looked like he was trying to hide something, he'd draw more attention than if he simply walked boldly and confidently among the Fireflies. Possibly, if no one was observing him, he could cover his robes with a layer of dust, as if he had just come out of the desert. But the desert was red and the dust of the city streets was brown; it might call even more attention to himself.

The best alternative was to return to the stable and wait there until the sun set the rest of the way. He was just about to do so when a caravan of Fireflies and their beasts of burden passed by, laden with exotic goods. There was a chance that there was another stable further up the road, that their animals would be quartered there, but it wasn't worth the risk of exposure if he guessed wrong.

A small insect landed on his cheek, and he instinctively slapped at it. One of the Fireflies, sitting atop its ugly mount, turned to stare at him.

What now? thought Lennox. *Didn't any of you ever take a swipe at an insect before?* And then he tried to remember: had *he* ever seen a Firefly react to an insect? He couldn't recall a single instance.

The Firefly was still staring at him, and he felt the need to do something, *anything,* to assuage what he was sure were its suspicions. He considered everything from faking a fit to eating the insect, and settled, uncomfortably, for meticulously readjusting the thick hood of his robe. He dared a quick look in the direction of the Firefly; evidently it had lost interest in him, and was once again staring dully at the street.

Still, just to be on the safe side, he began walking again, turning into the first side street he came to. It seemed to be a row of hovels housing weavers. There were great vats of dye, and large hanks of colorful yarn hanging out to dry. Here were the reds and oranges of the desert tribes, the muted browns and greens of the city dwellers, even the whites of the warrior caste and the golds of the priests. Firefly females sat at their looms, their fingers moving swiftly and surely, creating subtle patterns, while dozens of children played in the street. A small, feline creature emerged from a house and began walking across the street. One of the children threw a rock at it; it snarled and raced back inside.

As Lennox walked down the street, ignoring the children and ignored in turn by them, he saw an occasional water gourd hanging near a loom, and tried not to think about it. There was no way he could steal one without being noticed, not in an area as crowded as this. This led him to wonder if he was still sweating, then to lick his upper lip to find out. It was moist and salty. Were any sweat stains visible? He didn't know, and had no way to check on them, but the children continued to pay him no attention, so he assumed his outer robes were still dry.

He looked at a pair of male children chasing each other up the street. How the hell did they do it? Their metabolism couldn't be that different, not living as they did on an oxygen world that was capable of supporting human life. But they didn't sweat, they didn't drool, they didn't pant, they didn't give any indication that the heat affected them at all. Evolution and adaptation, he told himself, evolution and adaptation. But that didn't explain the wings. They couldn't fly—given their structures, they had *never* flown—so what were the wings for? And their fingers—why were they so long? How did useless wings and four-jointed fingers qualify as survival traits?

I should have done more homework.

But of course, that was precisely what he was doing *now*. The Fireflies had no use for Men. They refused to trade with them. They refused to exchange ambassadors. They refused to have anything to do with Man's sprawling Republic. They allowed Men one small outpost, right in the middle of that sun-baked southern desert known as Hell's Oven, but no Man was allowed access to their cities. Indeed, it was a minor miracle that Lennox had managed to learn their language, since there were no radio or video signals to study and analyze; he had accomplished it by being incarcerated with a Firefly who had killed four Men, and he had to fight for his life perhaps fifty times before the Firefly was willing to declare a truce and begin trying to converse with him. Even now, as he tried to pass for a Firefly and make his way to the pyramid, he was totally ignorant of the meaning behind the crude squiggles that passed for the Fireflies' written language.

The spoken language wasn't much better. Simplistic and crude, and grating to the ear—but there was a certain poetry to it when translated back into Terran. The Fireflies' name for Medina was Grotamana, which meant "Touched by God," while the city in which he found himself, Brakkanan, was, literally, "Gold at Day's End." There were some fifty-odd dialects just in this hemisphere, but fortunately the language he had learned from his cellmate was a bastard tongue that had become the lingua franca for thousands of miles in every direction.

A trio of flying insects began buzzing around his face. He tried to ignore them, and they were joined by half a dozen more.

It must be the salt, he decided. Now that he was prepared, he could control his reactions—but none of the Fireflies were being bothered by insects, and if he drew enough of them, someone would start wondering why.

He continued walking until he was well past the children, then turned a corner, surreptitiously ran his hand over the front of a filthy building, and covered his face with dirt and grime, hoping that it would mask the odor of his perspiration from the insects. He gave no thought to how it would affect his appearance; if any Firefly actually saw his face, clean or dirty, he was a dead man anyway.

The shadows began lengthening as the sun plummeted down behind the distant hills, and Lennox began to think he actually had a chance of accomplishing his goal. The temperature began dropping precipitously. It was still hot, and it would remain hot, but he no longer felt like he was in danger of melting. He hadn't lost his craving for water, but somehow, with the coming of the darkness, he was able to control it.

He considered approaching the pyramid. The streets were emptying, and he would have a clear path, unhindered by any Fireflies. But the very act of walking there alone would call too much attention to himself, and he had no idea what was expected of him once he arrived, so he kept to the shadows, hoping to remain unseen, and planning to fall in behind the first group of Fireflies who emerged from their dwellings to begin the mile-long trek.

He would have liked to have simply squatted down, his back propped against a wall, and feigned sleep for the next hour, but he had no idea if Fireflies slept in such positions—the Firefly he had been incarcerated with hadn't seemed to sleep at all—and he decided not to risk it. But the sudden silence and lack of movement convinced him that they also didn't walk around after dark, at least not until they went to the pyramid, so he simply stood in the shadows, motionless, and hoped that no one would see him.

Five minutes passed, then ten more—and then a lone Firefly came walking down the narrow street. Lennox stood still, trying to hide the tension in his body, and hoping to strike an attitude that implied that of course this was where he belonged.

The Firefly stopped when he was about ten feet away and stared intently at Lennox. Lennox looked at the ground, seemingly oblivious to him.

Finally the Firefly began walking again, and just as Lennox began to relax, he turned back and said something in a dialect that Lennox had never heard before.

Lennox continued staring at the ground and made no response. The Firefly walked back to him and repeated the phrase.

"I do not understand you," muttered Lennox in the one language he had mastered.

"You are not of the Realm or the Legion," said the Firefly, switching to the lingua franca.

"No, I am not," replied Lennox, wondering what he was talking about.

"Nor are you of the Seven."

"That is true," said Lennox.

"There is something different about you," said the Firefly. "You mangle the language and you do not meet my gaze."

"I was born unable to speak clearly," answered Lennox, "and I do not meet your gaze because I am ashamed of my shortcoming."

It seemed like a reasonable answer, but something about it was terribly wrong, because without another word the Firefly launched himself at Lennox, his hands reaching out to clutch at the human's throat.

Lennox was caught completely off-guard by the suddenness of the attack, and an instant later was struggling for his life as the Firefly's hands tightened around his neck. He delivered a swift knee to the groin, which would have disabled any human opponent, but had no effect whatsoever on the Firefly. A thumb to the armpit elicited a groan, but did not make the Firefly relinquish his hold. Lennox felt himself becoming dizzy as he gasped futilely for air. Spots began appearing before his eyes, and finally he decided the only chance he had of surviving was to match surprise with surprise. He swiftly moved a hand to his face and pulled at the scarf that covered it until it was fully exposed.

The Firefly's eyes widened. *"You are a Man!"*

Lennox used that instant to twist free. He didn't dare give his opponent time to think or call for help, and he instantly delivered a crippling kick to the Firefly's left knee. The Firefly grunted and fell to the ground and Lennox, his scarf in his hands, swiftly wrapped it around the Firefly's neck and began tightening it.

The Firefly struggled to free himself, furiously at first, then with ever-weaker efforts, until he finally lay still. Lennox made sure he was alive, then quickly dragged him to the darkest section of the street, where he bound and gagged him with his own scarves.

As quick and silent as the battle had been, Lennox still could not believe that Fireflies weren't pouring into the street to determine the cause of the commotion, and decided that, early or not, he would be safer approaching the pyramid than remaining where he was. Keeping to the shadows as much as possible, he began walking to the north, his eyes and ears alert to every motion and sound.

When he had left the city and covered half the distance, he heard the draft animals of a caravan off to his right. He hid behind a rocky outcrop and watched as they came into view. There were six Fireflies mounted atop their beasts, and they led a train of thirty more animals, all carrying heavy burdens, each tied halter-to-tail to the beast ahead of it. With the sun down, four of the Fireflies had their hands and heads exposed, and he stared in fascination. They may have been dull and lackluster by day, but because of some element in their skins they literally glowed by night.

He briefly considered cutting the last animal loose with his knife, slicing its cargo loose, and mounting it, but they were noisy, temperamental animals, and he didn't want to risk exposure if the creature should start its characteristic bleating.

Still, the caravan offered him some protection once they reached the blazing torches that surrounded the pyramid, and the tracks they made would cover his own footprints, so he waited until the first twenty animals had walked by and then quickly walked out from behind his outcropping and began walking alongside the twenty-first beast. Its head shot up and its eyes widened when it became aware of him, but it remained silent and continued walking. Lennox kept as close to it as he could, in case any of the six riders should chance to look back, but their attention was centered on the glowing torches up ahead.

The caravan came to a halt within a quarter mile of the pyramid, and Lennox slipped into the darkness just before one of the Fireflies walked down the row of animals to make sure none had broken loose. The Fireflies then exchanged low whispers and began walking down a path that was marked by torches.

Lennox watched as they got to within thirty feet of the base of the pyramid, genuflected, made a complicated gesture with their hands, and began slowly walking around it in a counterclockwise direction.

He looked about for some sign of a priest or leader, but the only Fireflies he could see were the six members of the caravan. It didn't make any sense. This was their holiest of holy places: there *had* to be more going on than a handful of Fireflies walking in a large circle.

And suddenly he became aware that there *was* more going on. The Fireflies from the village were approaching in force, thousands, perhaps tens of thousands of them. They were marching toward the pyramid in single file, and while they were still half a mile away, he quickly realized that he wouldn't be able to simply become a part of their procession as he had joined the caravan, for a number of them also bore torches, and if they kept to the same path as the caravan, they would not pass within sixty feet of him. He'd never be able to span the gap without being spotted.

He was faced with two options: he could wait until the last of them had passed and fall into step behind them, or he could approach the pyramid now, before they arrived. Since he had no guarantee that the last few Fireflies wouldn't be carrying torches, he decided upon the second alternative.

He walked briskly to the path the Fireflies all seemed to follow instinctively, then turned toward the pyramid and continued at a slower pace. When he reached the spot where the caravan members had genuflected, he did so too, and then tried as best he could to duplicate the gesture they had made with their hands. This done, he began circling the pyramid as he had seen the Fireflies do, shortening his stride to make sure he would not catch up with them.

As he continued circling to his left, passing out of sight of the horde from the village, he came to a stop and breathed a sigh of relief. *He'd made it!* All he had to do now was wait until the villagers started walking around the pyramid: he would pretend to stumble, allow a few of them to pass him, and then fall into step with them so that he would be able to duplicate whatever they did. Nothing to it. The worst was over.

He was still congratulating himself on his accomplishment when a golden-robed Firefly came out of the darkness, grabbed him by the shoulder, spun him around, and ripped the scarf away from his face.

"We have been expecting you, Xavier William Lennox," said the Firefly, and even though the high-pitched voice came from an alien throat, Lennox found the tones ominous.

Three more Fireflies suddenly appeared, threatening him with metal-tipped spears.

Lennox could think of no answer that would in any way mitigate his situation, so he simply stood still and made no reply.

"You have been repeatedly warned to stay away from this place," continued the Firefly. "You have been told that such an invasion of our privacy would not be permitted. And yet you have come. Why?"

"I was curious."

The Firefly emitted its equivalent of a contemptuous snort. It was an unpleasant sound.

TWO

❧❧❧❧❧❧❧❧❧❧❧

Lennox's hands were bound behind his back, and he was marched toward the immense pyramid he had come so far to see. It was some sixty feet tall, and its smooth golden sides were totally devoid of any markings or carvings. It amazed him that a race as primitive as the Fireflies could have constructed it. He toyed with the possibility that some other starfaring race had created and then abandoned it, and that over the eons its origin had been forgotten as it became the holiest of the Fireflies' many religious monuments.

"This is what you came for, is it not, Xavier William Lennox?" asked the golden-robed Firefly, gesturing toward the pyramid.

"I came to study the entire ceremony," replied Lennox truthfully.

"Why?"

"I was told that it is both beautiful and awesome."

"We have no desire to see *your* religious ceremonies," said the Firefly.

"You should attend one," said Lennox. "You might find it interesting."

"Your god allows any being of any race to attend?"

"Most of my people would argue that he is your god, too."

The Firefly uttered an alien chuckle. "They are welcome to think so."

"I would be happy to exchange religious views with you," offered Lennox.

"I'm sure you would," said the Firefly.

They came to a stop at the base of the pyramid.

"What do you plan to do with me?" asked Lennox, trying to hide his nervousness.

"You knew the consequences of your actions before you came here," replied the Firefly.

"Perhaps you had better consider the consequences of *your* actions," said Lennox, trying to imbue his voice with a tone of authority. "You cannot kill a Man without retaliation."

"You are in no position to make threats."

"I'm not here to harm anyone," replied Lennox. "I came alone and unarmed. Why not simply let me observe the ceremony and leave in peace?"

The Firefly stared at him for a long moment. "You are as single-minded and foolish as you were said to be."

Something between a grimace and a wry smile passed across Lennox's face. "It's my nature."

"Your nature is irrelevant."

Another Firefly, also wearing a golden robe, approached to within twenty feet of them and gestured Lennox's captor to approach him.

"You are surrounded," said the first Firefly. "Do not move or you will be instantly killed."

With that, he walked to the other gold-robed Firefly, and the two of them engaged in an animated discussion in a dialect that Lennox could not understand. Finally, after a few minutes, the first Firefly returned to him.

"You are quite fortunate, Xavier William Lennox," he said. "My people agree that killing you will bring repercussions upon us. This is of very little importance to me, for I know my god will protect us, but there are others whose faith is not as strong as mine. Therefore, if you will give me your word that you will leave Grotamana and never return, you will be permitted to live."

Son of a bitch! thought Lennox. *They bought it. They're not going to kill me!*

"You have it," replied Lennox, then added: "as soon as I have observed the ceremony."

"Your answer is unacceptable."

"You will find the weapons of my friends even less acceptable," replied Lennox meaningfully.

"We are many, you are few," noted the Firefly. "Perhaps we shall kill you all."

"If you do, then one day soon the sky will turn black with Republic ships, and not a single Firefly, not a single draft animal, not a single plant or flower will still be alive by nightfall."

"I have already explained that your threats are meaningless."

"I am not making a threat," answered Lennox. "I am making a prediction."

The Firefly left Lennox and approached his golden-robed companion. Again they engaged in an animated conversation for a moment, and then he returned.

"We are considering the situation."

Lennox nodded. "That is a wise thing to do." He paused. "Have you a name?"

"Why?"

"I wish to know whom to thank when I am released."

"My name is Chomanche, and you will not wish to thank me."

Suddenly the Fireflies fell silent and began looking up. Lennox did the same, and saw a naked Firefly, his skin glowing a pale gold in the dark, standing atop the pyramid.

"You will stay where you are until we have decided what to do with you," said Chomanche.

"Where would I go?" asked Lennox.

"Nowhere," said Chomanche decisively. He signaled to two of the armed Fireflies and uttered a brief command. Before Lennox could translate it and anticipate what was coming, each Firefly had thrust a spear through one of his feet.

Lennox bellowed in surprise and pain. He wanted to fall onto his knees, to do anything to take some of the pressure off his feet, but Chomanche held his bound hands firmly behind his back. Finally he nodded and the Fireflies withdrew their spears. It was even more excruciating than the initial thrusts. When Chomanche felt Lennox begin to collapse, he released his grip on the bonds and allowed the human to sink to the ground.

"You didn't have to do that!" grated Lennox, as blood poured out through the holes in his shoes.

"Of course we did," replied Chomanche calmly.

"I wasn't going anywhere!"

"You are not to be trusted."

Chomanche stepped a few feet away and shifted his gaze to the lone figure atop the pyramid, and, through a haze of pain, Lennox looked up.

The naked Firefly stood at the very edge, some sixty feet above them, making what Lennox assumed to be mystical signs with his hands. Suddenly his vestigial wings began flapping, the first time Lennox had ever seen any adult Firefly move the membranes on its back, and the assembled multitude began a deep, guttural, singsong chant. The wings beat faster and faster until Lennox could no longer make out their shape, and then, with no warning, it hurled itself straight out into space.

For just an instant Lennox thought it might actually fly, but then it began plummeting down, its wings still fluttering with blinding speed. Halfway down it careened off the side of the pyramid, shot out fifteen feet, and continued falling to the ground, where it landed with a sickening thud.

Soon a second Firefly appeared atop the pyramid, and the entire pageant was repeated until it, too, lay dead upon the ground.

Lennox waited for a third enactment, but after a moment he realized that the crowd was no longer looking up, and he assumed that this part of the ceremony—if that was the right name for it—was over.

Lennox tried to get to his feet, but the pain was too great, and he instantly fell to the ground, cursing. He forced himself to think about something else, anything else, to take his mind off the excruciating agony.

The ceremony. Concentrate on the ceremony. Try to make sense of it.

Ritual suicide? Probably not. He didn't know much about the Fireflies' culture, but suicide didn't jibe with the bits he *did* know.

His feet began throbbing as the blood continued to ooze out of them.

Concentrate!

If not suicide, then what? If the Fireflies didn't plan to die, then they must have thought they could fly. But of course they couldn't; their bones were too solid, their wings too flimsy, their entire structures wrong. But *if . . .*

Could it be a test for a messiah of sorts? That if one of them actually *did* fly, he would become the leader?

But that was ridiculous. Those wings had *never* been able to hold a Firefly body in flight. After eons of Fireflies diving to their death from atop the pyramid, they'd have to know none of them would stay airborne.

The pain began seeping back into his consciousness. He tried to fight it back.

Both of the plungers had been males. Did that have anything to do with it? And if so, *what* did it mean?

Or were they criminals? But why would criminals be involved in a religious ceremony?

Suddenly a Firefly in a gold robe—not Chomanche, but one he hadn't seen before—intruded on his thoughts by chanting in a high voice. Then, when the chant stopped, the entire assemblage began racing around the base of the pyramid.

Chomanche instantly grabbed Lennox by the back of

his robe and began dragging him away from the pyramid. A moment later the fastest of the Fireflies rounded a corner of the pyramid and raced over the spot where Lennox had been lying.

"Why did those two jump off the pyramid?" asked Lennox.

Chomanche summoned an armed warrior.

"Our prisoner insists upon asking questions," he said. "Take his mind off his curiosity."

The Firefly stepped behind Lennox, who struggled to turn and see what he was doing. Chomanche laid a heavy hand on his shoulder to hold him still. For a brief moment Lennox thought nothing could be worse than the uncertainty of what would happen next. Then a sharp blade came down across the fingers of his right hand, and as he fell to his side, cursing in agony, he knew he had been wrong, that the fact was worse than the anticipation.

"No more questions?" said the Firefly sardonically.

"You'd better kill me, you bastard!" snarled Lennox as blood gushed from the stumps where his fingers had been. "Because if you don't, I'll come back for you! I swear it!"

Chomanche made a clicking sound. "You are a very slow learner, Xavier William Lennox."

He nodded to the warrior, and Lennox felt an alien hand hold his left hand steady for a moment, and the blade came down again. Lennox bellowed an obscenity, almost fainted, bit his lip until the blood flowed freely, and glared silently at Chomanche.

"If I were you, Xavier William Lennox," said Chomanche, "I would hold my tongue while it was still in my head."

Lennox felt his wrists being tightly bound with a soft cloth. The cloth cut into them, causing them to bleed, but it was tight enough to cut off the flow of blood to his severed fingers. Then the ropes that held his hands behind him were severed, and he painfully moved his arms until his mutilated hands were in front of him. He wanted to clutch them, but realized that he no longer had anything to clutch them with. As the flow of blood stopped, he settled for crossing his arms and tucking his hands in his armpits.

Ceremonies were going on, prayers and chants were being uttered, glowing golden bodies were strutting in set patterns, but Lennox was oblivious to it all. He knew he was going to die, slowly and painfully, piece by piece, in greater agony than he had ever imagined in his worst nightmares. He concentrated on his hatred of Chomanche, which was the only thing that could even momentarily take his mind off his pain.

Two gold-robed Fireflies came up to Chomanche and whispered something to him. He nodded, replied, and turned to Lennox.

"You told me that you came alone."

"I did," muttered Lennox.

"You persist in lying to me," said Chomanche. "That is most unwise."

He nodded his head almost imperceptibly, and a sword came down from beyond Lennox's range of vision, severing the front half of his left foot. Blood spurted out and another scream escaped him as he almost lost consciousness.

"A party of twenty Men is approaching Brakkanan," continued Chomanche. "They can have only one reason, and that of course is to find you. When they are convinced you are not there, they will come here."

"I know nothing about them," whispered Lennox, as another tourniquet was applied to his left leg.

"We cannot let them come here," said Chomanche. "We would have to kill them all, and we have no desire to bring your Republic's ships to Grotamana. Therefore, they will find you halfway between Brakkanan and the pyramid, and, having found you, they will proceed no further."

"They will hunt you down," muttered Lennox.

"They will have two choices," answered Chomanche. "They can save your life, or they can try to exact their revenge while letting you die. Since they have come to find you, they will choose the former."

He nodded to two of the warriors, who each grabbed one of Lennox's ankles and began dragging him roughly across the dry, parched ground.

He had no idea how long they dragged him, or how far. He knew that almost all the skin had been torn from his back, and that his arms and left leg were in agony from the tightness of the tourniquets. He thought he could still hear the chants from the pyramid, but he was so dizzy and so nearly unconscious that he couldn't be sure he wasn't imagining them.

Finally they came to a stop, and the warriors released him. Both legs fell hard upon the ground, and he screamed again.

"It is here that your friends shall find you, Xavier

William Lennox," said Chomanche. "If you are very lucky, they may even be able to keep you alive."

Lennox didn't have the strength to reply.

"You have seen things this night that no member of your race may see," continued Chomanche. "We cannot change that, but we can remove the offending organs. Do you understand what I am saying to you?"

Lennox tried to get to his feet, felt an excruciating pain in what remained of his left foot, and collapsed. One of the warriors rolled him onto his back, and then each of them pinned an arm down on the ground, as Lennox struggled weakly and futilely to free himself.

"Relax, Xavier William Lennox," said Chomanche, kneeling down next to him. "Even if we let your hands loose, what could you do with them? Can you make a fist? Can you grip my arm and hold it back?"

Lennox struggled again, and one of the warriors used his free hand to hold the human's head still.

Suddenly a sharp instrument appeared in Chomanche's hand. Lennox hoped he would pass out before the hand came any closer, but he knew that he wouldn't.

THREE

He was unconscious for three days and delirious for two more. He had nightmares about glowing golden blades hacking away little pieces of his body. His fingers itched, but he didn't *have* any fingers. He tried to roll over and found that he was strapped to his bed. He seemed to think that he was tied into a battery of machines by a plethora of tubes and wires, but he couldn't open his eyes to see them.

Finally he became aware of a steady prodding against his shoulder. He wanted to tell whoever was bothering him to go away, that as long as he was asleep nothing hurt and that he could handle his nightmares but if he woke up he'd be faced with a terrible reality, that he wanted to sleep the rest of his life away. The prodding continued and his mouth was so dry that his tongue was stuck to the roof of it and he couldn't say anything without pulling it loose, and he didn't want any more pain, not even the mild discomfort of speaking. He moaned and tried to roll away, but the restraints held him motionless.

"The machines say you're awake, Mr. Lennox," said a feminine voice.

He lay perfectly still, hoping to lull the machines into making a mistake.

"You're lucky to be alive," continued the voice.

The nightmares vanished, to be replaced by the memories, which were worse.

"Define 'lucky,' " mumbled Lennox.

"If we'd found you ten minutes later, you'd be dead."

Lennox was too busy trying to erase the images of Chomanche's knife from his mind to reply.

"You were in a very bad way."

Now tell me something I don't know, thought Lennox.

"I see your eyelids fluttering, Mr. Lennox," said the voice. "Please don't try to open them. They've been sealed shut to prevent infection."

He suddenly felt an urge to wiggle his fingers and toes, and fought to resist it.

"Are you in any pain?" asked the voice.

He did a quick survey and found, to his surprise, that he *wasn't* in pain.

"I don't think so."

"That's because we've given you a very strong pain-blocker," said the voice. "It'll mask your pain, but shouldn't affect your perceptions. You'll be able to think clearly, once you adjust to your current circumstances."

"What *are* my circumstances?"

"You're in the infirmary of a Republic ship bound for Hippocrates, the medical research center that orbits Windsor V."

"That's *our* circumstances," he rasped. "What are *mine*?"

"You have been severely mutilated, Mr. Lennox," was the answer. "Part of your left foot was severed, and both feet seem to have been pierced with swords or spears. You are missing three fingers from your right hand and four from your left. Both of your eyes have been removed, and your left ear was sliced off. I am told that when you were found, you were pinned to the ground with a pair of spears that were run through your shoulders." The voice paused. "You have undergone three surgeries and four transfusions. It was necessary to amputate the rest of your left foot—infection had spread throughout it, and we were, after all, fighting to save your life—and we also had to remove the stubs of your fingers for the same reason. Evidently you'd been dragged through sand and dirt with these gaping wounds; it would have been impossible *not* to become infected."

"Were there any reprisals against the Fireflies?"

"I have no idea," replied the voice. "I don't even know what a Firefly is."

Lennox was silent for a moment. "How come I'm not hungry? It's been days since I've eaten."

"You're being fed intravenously."

"Are you my doctor or my nurse?"

"I'm *one* of your doctors. You've got six of them at the moment." A pause. "You're one of my most famous patients. I've read all four of your books.'' Another pause. ''You came across as a very grumpy traveler. If this is what you go through to get material for a book, I can understand why.''

Lennox frowned. ''I'm getting groggy.''

''Your system has had too many severe shocks, both on Medina and in surgery. You'll spend most of the next week sleeping.''

''My family . . .''

''They've been informed. They'll be waiting for you at Hippocrates.''

He was sure he had more questions to ask, but he was asleep before he could think of them.

FOUR

❧❧❧❧❧❧❧❧❧❧❧❧❧❧❧❧

Lennox had been home for five weeks. He spent most of his time dictating to his computer and editing the resultant manuscript. He left his house only for regular visits to the local hospital, where he pleased his doctors with the speed of his recovery and mystified them by his refusal to use any of the prosthetic devices they had given him except for one artificial eye.

He hired three nurses to serve eight-hour shifts, but within a month he no longer needed them, and replaced them with a rotating series of "personal companions," whose primary duties were to fix his meals, dress and bathe him, and act as a first line of defense against unwanted visitors.

After he finished the first two chapters of his latest book, he transmitted them to his agent, Angela Stone, a striking redhead who was also the second of his three ex-wives. He was not surprised when she showed up on his doorstep ten days later; he instructed his companion of the moment to usher her into his paneled study and then leave the two of them alone.

Angela, dressed in a business suit that seemed to change pastel shades as she moved, entered the room, and Lennox stared admiringly at her out of his single eye.

"You know, you're still a damned fine-looking woman," he said by way of greeting.

She stared at him without comment.

"You seem distrustful," he observed.

"I am."

"Can't I offer an honest compliment without you thinking I want something in return?"

"You never have before," she replied, opening her briefcase. She withdrew a thick contract and tossed it onto a table, then sat down across from Lennox.

"How am I expected to sign that?" he asked dryly.

"If you want the money, you'll find a way," said Angela with no show of sympathy. "You've got a whole roomful of prosthetics upstairs, Xavier. Playing the tragic hero may impress your adoring public, but *I* know better." He was about to answer, but she held up a hand. "It's been five weeks now," she continued. "You've already had the press photograph you in this disgusting state, and I'm sure you've got an absolutely revolting portrait ready for your dust jacket. Just out of curiosity, how much longer do you intend to act the crippled martyr before you finally use your new hands and feet?"

"After I make a couple of public appearances," said Lennox. "I'm giving a speech on Roosevelt III next week, and another one on Sirius V the week after. I think my appearance will reinforce what I have to say.''

''I doubt it,'' replied Angela. ''The critics are already having some difficulty deciding whether you want to be a scholar or a sensationalist.''

''Who says they have to be incompatible?'' asked Lennox. ''One pays for the other.''

''This is *me* you're talking to, Xavier,'' she said. ''I lived with you for three years, remember?''

''Serves me right for marrying my agent,'' he said wryly. ''You made me rich, and then took half my money when you left.''

''You're not an easy man to live with,'' she noted. ''I earned every credit of it.''

''So did my other wives,'' he replied with a rueful smile. ''That's why I see nothing wrong with sensationalism. I've got a lot of bills to pay, and you three ladies are sitting on all my ill-gotten gains.''

''Rubbish,'' she said. ''I *know* you, Xavier.''

''What is that supposed to mean?'' he asked.

''I mean this has nothing to do with money.'' She paused. ''I've read the chapters you sent me.''

''How did you like them?''

''They scared the hell out of me,'' she replied honestly. ''That's why I'm here.''

''Good! I haven't lost my touch.''

''That's not what I mean,'' she said. ''You're going back, aren't you?''

''Back?'' he repeated.

''To Medina.''

''After what they did to me?'' he said. ''You couldn't pay me enough to go back.''

"You don't do it for the money, Xavier," replied Angela firmly. "You never did."

"The hell I don't."

"You can lie to yourself, but you can't lie to me," she continued. "I know you too well. I used to think that you were just an overgrown boy, that you loved to go off on adventures, and that someday you'd grow up."

"You were wrong."

"I know," she said. "I was wrong about a lot of things. Thinking of you as an immature adventurer was too simplistic." She paused and stared at him. "I think you've only truly loved two things in your life, Xavier: yourself—and death." She smiled wryly. "Here you are, risking your life on all these alien worlds, and publishers actually pay you to do it." She uttered a short, dry laugh. "If they only knew you as I do, they'd *charge* you."

"The amateur psychiatrist strikes again," he shot back contemptuously. "Aren't you tired of analyzing me?"

"It goes hand-in-glove with knowing you," she replied seriously. "I've been doing it ever since our marriage started falling apart. If you'd been attracted to another woman, or even to a man, I would have known what to do, how to fight back. But I lost you to a series of nameless dangers on uncharted worlds. I didn't know how to compete with them, so I tried to find out why you were so obsessed by them."

"It's the way I make my living," he said. "None of you ever understood that."

She stared briefly at the various alien artifacts that lined the walls of the study, then answered him.

"Other men and women have made their livings visiting alien worlds and writing up their experiences. Only *you* feel compelled to continually put your life at risk."

"The reason my books sell so well is because I don't just dabble on the surface of things," he explained irritably. "I don't just *observe* the natives; I *live* with them. I share their food and their quarters, I learn their customs and their beliefs. When you're through with one of my books, you *know* what a world is like!"

"And you really think that's why people buy your books?"

"What other reason is there?"

"They're voyeurs, Xavier. They don't want to learn about aliens. They want your account of swallowing a live snake on Bareimus II, or that aberrant interspecies sexual escapade that got you kicked out of the Albion Cluster." She paused. "They won't give a damn about the Fireflies, but they'll buy a million copies of your next book just to read about your mutilation."

"I've had enough!" snapped Lennox angrily, slamming a hand down on the arm of his chair. "My books are *important*. Maybe I had to listen to all this shit when we were married, but I sure as hell don't have to now. If you don't like what I write, just say so and I'll get a new agent!"

"As long as your books sell, I'm your agent, and a damned good one at that," she shot back. "You owe me that much for all the hell you put me through."

"If you're not trying to end our business relationship, what the hell is this all about?"

"If you weren't so totally self-absorbed, you'd *know*

what it's about," said Angela. "I don't want you to go back to die on Medina."

"Is that my wife speaking, or my agent?" he asked sarcastically.

"Both," she said. "Your agent doesn't want her best source of income to dry up, and your ex-wife still feels some slight affection for you, God knows why."

"You make me sound like a psychological basket case." He held up his fingerless hands. "What I am is a *physical* basket case. Nothing could get me to go back there."

"Who do you think you're kidding?" said Angela. "I'm the woman you left behind to go to Jefferson III and New Ghana and Cinderblock. If your publisher gives you the tiniest excuse, you'll be packing your bags two minutes later."

Lennox shook his head adamantly. "Not this time. Those bastards cut me to ribbons."

"I know."

"They impaled me with their spears and left me for dead," he continued with an involuntary shudder. "And you think I'd go back after that?"

Angela paused for a moment before answering. "The truth?" she said at last. "I think you'd go back *because* of that."

"Not without protection."

"Then you *have* been thinking of it," she said accusingly.

"I've been thinking of what I did wrong," he said, flustered.

"And how to do it right the next time?" said Angela. "For God's sake, Xavier, there are bits and pieces of you rotting on three different planets! Isn't that enough?''

''You don't understand!'' he snapped. ''None of you have *ever* understood!''

''Then help me to,'' she said. ''Make me understand the attraction that a hideous death on an alien world holds for you.''

''You think I go there to die?'' he shouted at her. ''I go there to *learn*!''

''And what do you think you've learned?''

''Read my books,'' he said caustically. ''It's all there in black and white.''

''I *have* read them. All I've learned is that people who do foolish things usually pay a price for it.''

''They also accomplish things! Do you want me to sit in this room, staring at four walls, for the rest of my life?''

''Of course not.''

''Then what *do* you want?''

''I want you to write the books you're capable of writing,'' she said. ''But without trying to sneak into places humans are forbidden to go, and without participating in the ceremonies humans aren't even permitted to see.'' She paused and stared at him. ''Tell me, Xavier—have you ever gone to a world that *didn't* have taboos for you to break?''

''Sometimes it's necessary to get the story I want.''

''Like on Medina?''

''Precisely.''

''Then answer me this,'' said Angela. ''According to your manuscript, you had already stolen a copy of the Fireflies' holy book. Leaving aside the morality of stealing anyone's bible, once you got your hands on it, why was it necessary to risk your life going to the pyramid?''

''You can't understand a High Mass just by reading the New Testament,'' answered Lennox. He paused. ''I saw two Fireflies leap to their deaths from atop that pyramid, and I'll wager there's nothing in their bible that tells me why they did it.''

''I know. And it's precisely *what* you are willing to wager that I find so disturbing.'' She paused again. ''Don't you bear them any ill will at all for what they did to you?''

''Not really,'' said Lennox thoughtfully. ''You've got to understand that I was invading their territory against their wishes.''

''You shouldn't be trying to understand them, Xavier. You should either be doing your best to forget the incident ever happened, or else urging the navy to incinerate the whole damned planet. Your reaction isn't normal.''

Lennox shrugged. ''It feels normal to me.''

''I know. That's the problem.''

''It's an interesting culture.''

''It's a brutal, barbaric culture.''

''That's one of the things that makes it interesting.''

She sighed. ''I wish you found *people* half as interesting. You'd live a lot longer.'' She got to her feet. ''I suppose I should kiss you good-bye and tell you to come back with another best-seller, but I just can't bring myself to do that.'' She walked to the door, then turned to him. ''Just try not to act too irresponsibly when you go back to Medina.''

''I told you: I'm not going back.''

"I know," she replied. "But when you do, remember what I said."

She turned and left the room.

Lennox stared at the door for a moment, then shrugged as if to physically remove the annoyance of the past few minutes. Finally he turned to the computer and ordered it to bring up yet another text on Medina.

FIVE

Lennox had just finished giving his speech on Sirius V. Even he had to admit it had been impressive. He'd held the audience in the palm of his hand, describing his adventures on Medina in vivid detail. Now it was time for the question-and-answer session, and he called upon a young woman toward the front of the audience.

"What attracts you to these exotic alien worlds?" she asked.

Standard Answer Number 3, he thought to himself, as he wondered how soon the banquet would begin.

Aloud he said: "As a young boy I always wanted to see what lay beyond the next hill. Now I want to see what lies beyond the next star system." He paused. "There are thousands of fascinating worlds out there. Has anyone here ever been to Doradus?" There was no response. "Well, *I* have. The inhabitants never stand still. They have these incredibly long, stiltlike legs, and they follow the sun over the horizon, never stopping, never resting, never experiencing the dark. They mate, they give birth, they love and hate and grow old without ever halting in their endless trek.

"And there are the Brozians of Namatos VI. They reproduce by budding, just like vegetables. They've never developed computers—in fact, they have yet to develop a written language—and yet they've created a new branch of mathematics that less than a dozen Men have been able to grasp. And there are the Djebels, intelligent reptiles who have created a complex, functioning society despite the fact that they become comatose when the temperature drops.

"How can one know about such places and beings and *not* want to see them at first hand?"

His answer received polite applause, as it always did, and then a man seated over to the side stood up.

"If you have such respect for alien races, why do you constantly break their laws?"

"I have never broken an alien law," replied Lennox firmly.

"Let me rephrase that, then," persisted the man. "Why do you behave in a manner that you know is contrary to their wishes?"

Who let this idiot in? I thought they were supposed to screen the questions.

"If we're ever to live in harmony with our fellow beings," he said, thinking half a sentence ahead, "it is essential that we understand them. It is not enough to know that they do not desire our presence. We must learn *why* they feel that way, so that we can adjust our behavior to such a degree that we will no longer be un-welcome.''

''But doesn't invading their privacy reaffirm their desire not to have anything to do with us?''

''It's not that simple,'' answered Lennox. ''The Republic is the dominant force in the galaxy, and these races are going to come into contact with us whether they like it or not. The more we can learn about them, the more we can behave in such a manner that they eventually learn to accept us.''

I sound like an idiot! Why do they keep letting him follow up with more questions?

An elderly man stood up to ask about the Fireflies' social structure, and Lennox gratefully answered him at considerable length. He then apologized for cutting the session short, explaining that he had not yet fully recovered his strength, and joined his hosts for cocktails until the start of the banquet.

He had his usual difficult time eating without the use of his fingers, but a lovely blonde cut his food for him and fed him as if he were a baby. Half of him reveled in the attention, while the other half found the situation totally ridiculous and more than a bit demeaning.

He was as charming and gracious as the situation required, and made a short after-dinner speech that was really just a plug for his forthcoming book. Then, again using his health as an excuse, he announced that he wished to retire to the suite his sponsors had provided, where he had every intention of spending the next few hours reading or watching some mindless entertainment. He had hoped to make his exit using a pair of crutches—that was usually good for a newstape holo—

but they had provided him with a mobile chair and he rode it to the airlift, then ascended some thirty levels to his suite. The blonde made sure that he got there, but didn't offer to come in with him, and he decided it was no great loss.

He entered the sumptuous parlor and ordered the curtains to part, revealing the frigid, airless surface beyond the protective dome. He then contacted room service and told them to send up a bottle of Alphard brandy and charge it to his sponsors.

He pulled a prosthetic hand out of his luggage, used it to get out of his formal attire, then took a dryshower and changed into a more casual outfit. When he emerged from the bedroom he found that the brandy had already been delivered, and he poured himself a glass.

The room's security system informed him that he had a visitor, and, assuming that the blonde had returned and wondering vaguely if he was pleased or displeased about it, Lennox removed the prosthetic hand, stuck it beneath his chair, and ordered the door to open. It slid back, revealing a small, chunky, middle-aged woman in a severely cut gray business suit that almost matched the color of her hair.

"Mister Lennox?" she said.

"Yes. Who are you?"

"My name is Nora Wallace. May I come in?"

Lennox shrugged. "Why not?"

"Thank you," she said, entering the parlor as the door closed behind her.

"I don't remember seeing you in the audience," observed Lennox.

"I wasn't there."

"If you're here to give me my fee, it's supposed to be deposited in my account."

She ignored his statement and walked over to the bottle of brandy.

"From Alphard!" she said, impressed. "I haven't had an Alphard brandy in, oh, it must be four years now. Maybe five. Do you mind?"

"Help yourself."

"Thank you." She filled a small glass. "May I sit down?"

"Whatever makes you happy," said Lennox, staring at her. "You *are* eventually going to tell me who you are and why you're here, aren't you?"

"Certainly," said Nora Wallace, sitting down on a chair that floated gently a few inches above the floor. She sipped the brandy. "Ah! It's as good as I remember!"

He stared at her silently.

"Won't you join me?" she said. "Please feel free to use whatever prosthetic device you employed to open and pour it."

Lennox grinned, pulled the artificial hand out from where he had hidden it, quickly attached it, and picked up his glass.

"To Medina," she said, lifting her own glass.

"What about Medina?" he asked sharply.

"It's a fascinating world."

"I know."

"And an important one."

He stared at her. "Just who the hell are you?"

Nora tossed a titanium identification card to him.

"I'm the assistant secretary of the Department of Alien Affairs. My specialty is the Quinellus Cluster."

He made no reply.

"Medina is in the Quinellus Cluster," she continued.

"I know where it is."

"You look annoyed, Mister Lennox," she noted with amusement.

"If your department thinks they're going to censor anything I have to say or write about Medina . . ."

"We're not in the censorship business."

"Then you want me to add something, or perhaps slant the material."

"What you write is a matter of complete indifference to us, Mr. Lennox."

"Then what *do* you want?"

"That's what I'm here to talk about," said Nora, taking another sip of her brandy. "I heard you speak on Roosevelt III last week. I think your experiences were remarkable." She paused. "I also think they were incomplete."

"How much more of me did you want chopped off?" he asked sarcastically.

Nora Wallace smiled. "I admire your sense of humor, Mister Lennox. It must be very difficult to joke about what happened to you."

"I assume there's a point to all this?"

"Certainly." She paused. "How would you like to go back to Medina?"

"Seriously?" he said, surprised.

"I didn't come all this way to be facetious, Mister Lennox," she replied.

Don't let her see how eager you are. Only a crazy

*man would want to go back, and the government doesn't
deal with crazy men.*

"The Department of Alien Affairs doesn't have a
military arm," he noted. "And I'm a marked man on
Medina."

"What if I told you that we have ways of protecting
you?" she persisted. "Would you be interested?"

"It's possible," he said noncommittally. "What's
your interest in Medina?"

"Our geological surveys tell us that there are at least
six, and possibly as many as eight, diamond pipes in the
desert to the east of the city known as Brakkanan. The
Republic wants to set up a mining operation."

"The Fireflies will never permit it."

"Even if we offer them a lease agreement that stipu-
lates a percentage of the profits?"

What the hell is she talking about? Where do I fit in?

"It would be meaningless to them," replied Lennox.
"They still operate on a barter economy. Credits are just
so much useless paper to them."

"That's our department's conclusion as well," said
Nora. "Would you like to know the Republic's response?"

"I can guess."

"You don't have to guess, Mister Lennox," she said.
"They have given the Department of Alien Affairs one
year to get the Fireflies to agree to a lease."   •

"And if they refuse?"

"Then the navy will move in with as much force as is
required to pacify the natives and protect our mining operation."

"Pacify," repeated Lennox, unable to keep the con-

tempt from his voice. "A polite euphemism for genocide."

"In essence." She leaned forward. "That's why I
have been authorized to seek you out. I've heard you
speak about Medina, and you seem to bear the Fireflies
no malice—but to be perfectly honest you are a master-
ful showman, and I have no idea what your true feelings
might be."

"Even if you *can* protect me, I'm the last Man they'd
listen to."

"We're operating in a very limited time frame, and
you know more about the Fireflies than any other Man.
Also, as far as I have been able to ascertain, you're one
of the few Men who speaks their language fluently."

"They've got hundreds of languages and dialects,"
said Lennox. "I speak only one."

"The one they speak in Brakkanan, right?" she
asked.

"Yes."

"Well, there you have it. We'll be dealing with the
Brakkanan Fireflies."

"I'm curious to know how you expect me to negotiate with them when they probably have orders to kill me
on sight."

"I told you: we have means of protecting you."

*You'd better be right—because if you make the offer,
there's no way I'm going to refuse.*

"This is a society with a warrior caste. Anything less
than a heavily armed regiment will be ineffective." He
paused. "And if you've got a regiment handy, then you
don't need me. So what's the deal?"

Nora smiled. "If you agree to work for us, you will return to Medina alone and unarmed."

Lennox laughed harshly. "Lady, you're crazier than I am!"

Quick correction: almost no way.

"You are quite right that if we wanted to use force, we'd have no need for you, Mister Lennox. We want you because of your intelligence and your experience." She stared at him for a moment. "If you agree," she concluded, "we propose to invest more than one hundred million credits in you."

"That's enough!" he snapped irritably. "I thought you were making a legitimate offer. What kind of stupid joke is this?"

"I beg your pardon?"

"None of my books has ever earned as much as two million credits, and suddenly you're going to pay me fifty times that much? I don't know who put you up to this, but you're wasting my time."

"You misunderstand me, Mister Lennox," she explained patiently. "I didn't say we would *pay* you one hundred million credits. You will get rich enough selling a book based on your experiences—and I guarantee that your experiences will be the stuff of best-sellers. I said we would *invest* the money in you."

"I don't know what you're talking about."

"You will," Nora assured him.

"So I'm expected to just walk in there, negotiate, and walk back out without anyone laying a finger on me?"

"I said that we have the means to protect you," answered Nora. "I did *not* say that the mission was without risk."

"I don't mind a reasonable amount of risk," said Lennox. "It goes with the territory and makes good reading."

"Then may I assume that you *are* interested in returning to Medina if I can show you that you will not be subjected to an immediate attack?"

"You say that as if you're anticipating a delayed attack," he noted wryly.

"That will depend entirely upon you, Mister Lennox."

He poured himself another brandy. "All right, let me see if I've got this straight so far. You want me to return to Medina and try to talk the Fireflies into allowing the Republic to begin mining operations. You're spending a hundred million credits to safeguard my mission, yet I'm to operate alone, with no military support. If I survive, you're willing to let me write about my experiences and sell them. Have I got it right so far?"

"Yes. Are you interested?"

Suddenly he grinned at her. "Hell, yes!" he said. "Now, just how do you think you're going to protect me?"

"I was coming to that." She leaned forward. "We'll have to move fast, because the Republic hasn't given us very much time."

"That might be a problem," said Lennox.

"Oh? Why?"

"Look at me," said Lennox. "I could be half a year just learning how to use all the prosthetic devices that are waiting for me at home."

Nora Wallace smiled. "Forget about them, Mister Lennox," she said. "We have other plans for you."

SIX

❧❧❧❧❧❧❧❧❧❧❧❧❧❧

Lennox stopped a few feet away from the table and stared intently at the body of the Firefly.

"Is it real?" he asked.

"Absolutely," said the tall, angular woman in the white laboratory smock.

"Where did you get it?"

"From Medina, of course."

"I know that," said Lennox irritably. "I meant, *how* did you get it?"

"Don't concern yourself with details, Mister Lennox," said the woman. She stared down at the Firefly's body. "They're remarkable creatures, aren't they?"

Lennox made no reply. He noticed a tightening in the pit of his stomach.

"Interesting musculature," continued the woman. "And for the life of me, I simply cannot understand the vestigial wing structure. These creatures never flew at any point in their evolutionary history.''

''Let's grant that Fireflies are unique and wonderful and awe-inspiring. Nora Wallace told me that you would explain the process, Doctor . . .''

''Doctor Ngoni,'' came the reply. ''Since we're going to be working closely together for an extended period, I have no objection to you calling me Beatrice.''

''I don't know for a fact that we're going to be working together for more than this afternoon,'' said Lennox. ''If you can make Nora Wallace's scheme sound plausible, you'd better start doing so right now.''

''I'll do my best,'' said Beatrice Ngoni, conducting Lennox to the next room, which contained a desk, a pair of computers, and a trio of chrome chairs. ''Won't you sit down?''

Lennox seated himself on one of the chairs, while Beatrice Ngoni sat down behind her desk.

''I'm still waiting,'' said Lennox.

''I know,'' she said. ''I'll tell you what I can, but you must understand that the process is as new to us as it is to you.''

''I doubt it,'' said Lennox. ''I never heard of it until last night.''

''That doesn't mean that anything we plan to do isn't simply an extension of things we've done before,'' she continued, ignoring his comment. ''As you know, I am a reconstructive surgeon. Under other circumstances, I would be repairing the damage done to your body and fitting you with various prostheses. In a way, that's precisely what I *will* be doing over the next few months.''

''But you've never done *this* before.''

She smiled. "No human has ever had to pass for a Firefly on Medina before."

"I mean, you've never remade a Man into an alien?" he persisted.

She shook her head. "No. But we've fitted men out with unique prosthetic devices that have been designed to help them in their occupations."

"All right," said Lennox. "Tell me what's involved in the process."

"Didn't Nora Wallace already explain it to you?"

"Nora Wallace is a bureaucrat with her own agenda," said Lennox. "I want to hear it from the surgeon who's in charge of the operations."

"As you wish, Mister Lennox," she said, exhaling deeply. "First, we will have to remove your arms and legs. The musculature and joints are all wrong. They will be replaced by prosthetic limbs that are identical to those of a Firefly. We will also shorten your torso and redesign your hip joints. The greatest amount of surgery will be on your face, since it will be exposed at all times. We'll have to reshape the cheekbones and the jaw, eliminate the nose completely, give you eyes the same color as a Firefly's, elongate the skull, and eliminate all facial hair, even those in your nostrils and ears."

Lennox frowned. "How much of *me* will be left?"

"The essential you—your brain, your central nervous system, and your heart—will remain unchanged. We're not sure about your internal organs yet. You'll keep them, of course, but we may have to add a few artificial ones."

"Artificial organs?" he said. "Why?"

"To help you cope with the heat and the lower oxygen content of the air,'' she explained. ''We'll have to remove most of your sweat glands, though we'll probably allow you to sweat through your feet. We'll have to change your metabolism, too; you're going to have to eat and drink what Fireflies eat and drink, or you will call too much attention to yourself.'' She paused. ''We'll also give you some muscular control of your wings. The tricky part will be the skin. You describe it as appearing normal in the sunlight yet able to glow in the dark. I gather it is not an involuntary reaction, since according to your manuscript not all Fireflies glow at night. Unfortunately, the three specimens I have examined are no longer capable of glowing. I don't know what triggers it. To be truthful, I don't even know exactly what it looks like. If we can't come up with some harmless chemical coating and a means of distributing it over your body when you're being observed, it's entirely possible that we may have to give you an artificial epidermis as well.''

''So what you're saying is that you're going to replace my arms, legs, and skin, and redesign the rest of me?'' Lennox grimaced. ''That's more than *they* did.''

''We're also going to have to replace your genitals, Mister Lennox,'' she said. ''They are totally different from those of a Firefly.''

''Now just a minute . . .''

''What's the point of doing all the other surgery if you still have a human's genitals?'' she replied.

Lennox was silent for a moment. ''Before we go any farther, let me ask the operative question,'' he said. ''Assuming I return alive from Medina, can you put me back the way I was?''

"Well, yes and no," said Beatrice Ngoni.

"What the hell does *that* mean?"

"We won't be able to reattach your own limbs and genitals, and it's possible you may not be able to grow a new epidermis if we totally remove the old one. But we will be able to rebuild you with totally functional limbs and genitals. We will attach them to your neural passageways, and you will be able to function normally in every respect."

"In *every* respect?" repeated Lennox meaningfully.

"Including sexually," she replied. "In fact, you may well consider the end result a decided improvement. We can make you stronger, faster, and healthier than you were, and you'll have the added advantage of knowing that you will never again break a limb."

"You're sure?"

She smiled. "Turning you into a Firefly is the difficult part. Believe me, if we can do that, we can certainly turn you back into a Man."

"You said 'if,' " noted Lennox. "What's the downside?"

"That should be obvious. The downside is that you'll die on the operating table—or perhaps that you'll survive the surgery but give yourself away on Medina." She paused. "You were very fortunate to be rescued last time, Mister Lennox. I think it's safe to say that by the time we get through with you, no human will endanger his own life to rescue what you have become."

He considered her answer for a moment. "How many operations are we looking at here?"

"Seven, possibly eight, depending on the epidermis," answered Beatrice Ngoni. "Each operation will take approximately ten hours, and will require a team of between six and eight surgeons.''

''And the schedule?''

''That will depend upon your resiliency,'' she replied. ''Personally, I'd like to give you a month to recover from each surgery, but I gather that will not be possible, given the Republic's deadline. If you're up to it, we'll probably schedule one operation every ten to fourteen days. Then there will follow a recovery period, during which time you will have to learn how to function in your new body. The Department of Alien Affairs insists that you leave for Medina as soon as possible.'' She paused again. ''First, though, before we begin any surgical procedures, you'll be questioned extensively, under hypnosis, for at least a week.''

''Why?''

''We need to know everything that *you* know about Fireflies, including things you may have forgotten. For example, we have no idea what a Firefly sounds like when it speaks, so we have no idea how to adjust your vocal chords.''

''I don't need hypnosis to tell you that.''

''Perhaps not—but there are thousands of other details. For example, have you ever seen a Firefly sneeze or cough or blink? Do they have any involuntary reflexes, minor things you might have seen but which made little or no impression on you at the time? When they tire, do they pant? When they sleep, do they snore? How acute is their hearing? Their sense of smell? You spent time in a prison cell with one of them: how did he urinate and defecate?''

''All right, all right, I see the need for it.''

"Fine," she said. "Have you any other questions?"

"Just one. What, in your professional opinion, are the odds that the operations will be successful?"

"Define 'successful.'"

"Will I survive?"

"I'd say you have a seventy percent chance of survival."

"And will I be able to pass for a Firefly?"

"That's a chancier proposition. Although we've never performed such extensive cosmetic surgery before, there is no reason why it shouldn't work. But of course, whether or not you pass inspection ultimately depends on *you,* Mister Lennox. We can make you look like a Firefly, but only you can act like one—or fail to do so." She shrugged. "You may be able to live among them for months, or you may give yourself away in the first minute of contact."

Lennox was silent for a long moment as he tried to assimilate everything she had told him. Finally he stared across the table at her.

"Doctor Ngoni, what would you do in my place?"

"Given the treatment you've already received at their hands," said Beatrice Ngoni, "I think it's ridiculous to even consider placing yourself in their power again. However . . ."

"However?"

"I've seen your psychological profile."

"Oh?"

"It suggests that you are an exceptionally willful, stubborn, self-centered man who thrives on the unique hazards of his profession and possesses only a minimal sense of survival. My understanding is that the more I discuss the dangers of both the surgery and your mission, the more eager you will be to undergo them.''

"You remind me of one of my ex-wives," remarked Lennox wryly.

"I beg your pardon!" she said heatedlly.

"I didn't mean to offend you," said Lennox. "It's just that both of you seem to be of the opinion that I should be wearing a straitjacket."

"In the end, you might find it more comfortable than wearing a Firefly's body," said Beatrice Ngoni. "On the other hand, I suppose I should add that I consider your psychological profile to be the very type that promises the greatest likelihood of success."

"Why should you say that?" asked Lennox curiously.

"Because obsession will work to your advantage. If physical mutilation didn't stop you, I see no reason why the discomfort and dangers of physical transformation should."

"My feelings precisely."

She withdrew a single sheet of paper from a desk drawer. "I want you to read this before you leave."

"What is it?" he asked, staring at it.

"A release absolving the hospital and the Department of Alien Affairs of any responsibility should you die during surgery or in the course of your mission." She paused. "And now, have you any further questions?"

"Just one," said Lennox. He flashed her a disarming smile. "Do you have a pen?"

SEVEN

❦❦❦❦❦❦❦❦❦❦❦❦

*S*hit!"

Lennox tumbled heavily to the floor and lay there, panting.

"Are you all right, Mr. Lennox?" asked Beatrice Ngoni.

"No, I am not all right!" snapped Lennox. "I hurt in places I didn't even know I had." He paused, frowning. "You wouldn't think it'd be this hard to learn to walk with a Firefly's legs. *They* don't seem to have any trouble doing it."

"They've had their whole lives to practice," she replied. "You've walked like a Man for thirty-four years, and you're not quite halfway to being a Firefly even now." She stood before him. "Can you get up by yourself?"

"Of course I can get up by myself!"

"Well, then?"

"I'm resting."

"You'll have plenty of time to rest after the next operation," she said. "It's essential that you begin mastering your new body."

"I am."

"You are sprawled on the floor."

"I'm adjusting to my new vision," he said. "*You* try getting used to a world where all the blues have turned to gray and you're seeing two new colors plus a bunch of infrared waves."

"It shouldn't change your perception of shape and distance," remarked Beatrice.

"No, but it takes some getting used to."

He got unsteadily to his feet.

"Be careful," said Beatrice. "You're leaning too far forward."

He adjusted his position as best he could. "Why are they jointed like this?" he asked in frustration, indicating his legs. "What purpose does it serve?"

"The Fireflies didn't evolve the way Men did," she replied. "They were never arboreal. Once you learn to balance, you'll find that you can run far faster on these legs than you ever could on your own."

"Were they predator or prey?" asked Lennox.

She shrugged. "I have no idea. Probably both, at one time or another." She paused. "Are you ready?"

He nodded.

"All right," she said. "Begin walking counterclockwise around the room again."

Lennox started walking in an awkward gait. "When

am I going to get my new hands?'' he asked. ''I have this urge to clutch at things to keep from falling.''

''Next week,'' she answered. ''It's better that you learn to walk without them. I'm sure that Fireflies don't constantly grab things to keep their balance, and I don't want you to get into the habit.''

He spent another hour practicing with his new legs, then broke for lunch.

''How does it taste?'' asked Beatrice, as an attendant spoon-fed him the mushlike porridge that served as the Fireflies' staple diet.

''I can handle it,'' he replied.

''That's not good enough, Mr. Lennox,'' she said. ''I've read your books, and I'm well aware of the fact that you've eaten far less palatable things. However, for our purposes, it's essential that you not only eat it but *like* it.''

''That's going to take some doing.''

''I'm quite serious,'' said Beatrice. ''We'll make various adjustments to your taste buds until you *do* like it.''

''It's not necessary,'' replied Lennox. ''I can eat it like this.''

''You're not thinking, Mr. Lennox,'' she persisted. ''We do not anticipate that you will eat many meals alone, not if your mission is to succeed. If you are given spoiled food, or bitter food, or food that in any way offends the Firefly palate, and only *you* do not notice or protest, you could give yourself away.'' She paused and stared at him. ''*Now* do you understand?''

He sighed and nodded. ''Do what you have to do.''

''I always intended to.''

* * *

Lennox cursed aloud as he failed again.

"Try once more, please," said Beatrice Ngoni.

"Firefly males don't sew garments, so why the hell should they know how to thread a needle?" he asked irritably.

"It's a simple hand-eye coordination exercise," she replied. "You'll undergo several more before you're ready."

"It's so chilly in here it's hard to hold my hands steady," he said.

"Good," said Beatrice. "I was hoping you'd notice."

"What's the temperature?"

"Twenty-three degrees Celsius."

He turned to her. "You're kidding!"

"I'm quite serious." She smiled at him. "You're becoming a Firefly, Mister Lennox."

He awoke to the sound of gibberish. He shook his head to clear it, then opened his eyes and found himself facing a uniformed man.

"Good morning, Mister Lennox," said the man. "I am Major Luis Eduardo Belmonte." He smiled. "We are to be constant companions from this moment until you leave for Medina."

"We are?" said Lennox groggily. "Why?"

"Because I speak the Brakkanan dialect. Not as well as you, I am sure, but well enough to understand it and to make myself understood. These are the last words I will utter to you in Terran, and from this moment until you leave for Medina you will speak only in the dialect." He shifted languages. "Is that quite clear?"

"Quite," replied Lennox in the Brakkanan dialect.

"Good," said Belmonte. "It has been suggested that we attach a device to you that will give you a mild . . . ah . . . shall we say, *correction,* every time you revert to Terran. Will you consent to this?"

"How mild?"

"Speak only in the dialect and you will never know."

Lennox considered it, then nodded his acquiescence. "Yes, I consent to it."

"Excellent," said Belmonte. "I gather that the surgery on your larynx, tongue, and lips will not take place for another six days, so I don't expect perfect enunciation or inflection from you until that time."

"My language skills have already passed muster on Medina," said Lennox. "You'll have to accept my word for it. You're hardly the one to judge me; you've got an accent I could cut with a knife."

"A point well taken," agreed Belmonte. "At any rate, from this moment on you will speak to the hospital staff only through me."

"Fine," responded Lennox. "How long were you stationed on Medina?"

"I was there for almost five years. It took me that long to learn what little of the Brakkanan dialect I know. I envy you your language skills."

"Were you there when I had my little misadventure?"

Belmonte shook his head. "No, I was on furlough. But I heard about it." He paused. "I still can't believe that *anyone* made it to the pyramid!"

"As it turned out, making it there was easier than making it back," remarked Lennox wryly.

"I understand you've already written a few chapters about your experiences on Medina," said Belmonte. "I wonder if I could read them sometime?"

"They're in the computer," answered Lennox, gesturing to the glowing cube that sat on his desk. "Be my guest."

"Thank you," said Belmonte. "I look forward to it." He wiped some sweat from his brow and loosened his military tunic. "They keep it awfully warm in here, don't they?"

"I hadn't noticed," said Lennox truthfully.

"Is it working?" asked Lennox as he tried to flutter the translucent membranes that sprouted out from where his shoulder blades had once been.

"Just slightly," replied Belmonte.

"I can't feel them at all," complained Lennox.

Belmonte translated his statement for Beatrice Ngoni.

"That's because they're artificial constructs, and you're using muscles you never used before." She paused. "In fact, muscles you never *possessed* before."

"Then how do I—"

"It's just a matter of trial and error until you figure out how to manipulate them."

Lennox concentrated.

"Did anything move this time?" he asked.

"Not yet."

He tensed and grunted. "How about now?"

Belmonte shook his head. "All you're doing is flexing your shoulders."

"I'm using every muscle I have," complained Lennox. "They must have been attached wrong."

"Just keep trying."

He made another effort.

"Nothing," said Belmonte.

"Damn! I'll never get them to move."

But eventually he did.

"What do you think of it?" asked Belmonte, indicating the Firefly food that Lennox was eating.

"Pretty good, actually."

"How does it compare to human meals?"

"It's not steak, but it'll do."

At dinner Lennox was given a steak. He took two bites and promptly vomited.

"I think we're making progress," said Belmonte, as Lennox glared at him furiously through his orange alien eyes.

"All right," said Beatrice Ngoni. "Let's try out your new voice."

"Ready when you are," said Lennox.

She turned questioningly to Belmonte.

"There's something just a little wrong with the tone," he said.

"In what way?"

Belmonte frowned. "It should be . . . *deeper* isn't the word . . . more *resonant*."

"Give me a while," said Lennox. "I've only spoken one sentence."

"Any better?" asked Beatrice.

"I can't be sure," replied Belmonte.

"I want you to speak to him all afternoon, until his voice gives out," she said. "If at any point the pitch and tone seem right to you, call me immediately. We'll record the entire session. Once we know exactly how it should sound, we can make minor adjustments during the next surgery.''

"I can't speak all afternoon,'' protested Lennox. "My throat hurts already.''

Beatrice waited for Belmonte to translate, then turned to Lennox.

"Your throat is sore from the surgery, not from speaking the Brakkanan dialect. As you become tired, your voice will vary in pitch and strength. All we need is for Major Belmonte to let us know when it sounds proper, even for just a sentence or two, and we can make any correction that is required.''

"So what would you like to talk about?'' asked Belmonte when the two of them were alone.

"Torture.''

"Torture?'' he repeated, surprised. "Do you have any victim in mind?''

"Let's start with Beatrice Ngoni.''

His new teeth came next, followed by two internal organs whose function remained a mystery to him. He spent several sessions adjusting to his night vision, which was far superior to that of humans. His new ears were capable of hearing high-pitched sounds that were beyond the range of human hearing.

The next-to-last surgery replaced his genitals—he had been allowed to keep them as long as possible for psychological reasons—and he surprised everyone by not showing the least discomfort or dismay over his new spikelike sex organ.

The glowing skin remained a problem, and eventually it was decided to give him an entirely new epidermis, with internal triggers that could increase or moderate the degree of brightness; it took him almost two weeks to learn how to work the triggers. Finally they implanted yet another artificial organ, one that could absorb the phosphorescent secretion through his artificial skin whenever he willed it. That took him another ten days to master.

But finally, after slightly more than five Galactic Standard months, the newly minted Firefly named Xavier William Lennox was deemed ready for duty, and boarded a ship for distant Medina.

His excitement at returning to the planet was only minimally greater than his happiness at leaving Beatrice Ngoni and her colleagues behind.

EIGHT

❦❦❦❦❦❦❦❦❦❦❦

The first thing he noticed was that, although there were no clouds in the pale sky and the sun was beating down directly upon him, he felt mildly warm rather than unpleasantly hot. As he began walking across the desert, the soles of his feet became moist but not uncomfortable, and he marveled at how easily his new body was able to negotiate both the sand and the distance.

This is some body. I've walked ten, maybe twelve miles in the blazing sun, and it's not the least bit tired. I could get used to this.

He had a canteen hidden beneath his robes, but even after two hours of walking in the midday sun he felt no need to drink. His artificial eyes scanned the horizon with the precision of binoculars, looking for signs of habitation. There weren't any, but he saw an oasis about ten miles away and headed for it.

Along the way he came across a large insect, almost two inches long, that reminded him of a scarab. His human instincts told him to avoid it, but his curiosity prompted him to catch it with his long, slender fingers. A pair of pincers suddenly emerged from the insect's head and attempted to grab his hand. He quickly crushed the head and then, because the abdomen felt full and soft, he pierced it with a long, iron-hard fingernail. Liquid poured out onto his fingers. He threw the insect away and tasted the residue. His brain told him it was disgusting; his body told him that it tasted good, and that it was all the liquid he would need until he reached the oasis.

When he was three miles away, he saw a dozen beasts of burden, and a moment later he could make out the three Fireflies that were sitting beneath a shade tree. His first thought was to turn away, but they doubtless had seen him too, and besides, he was here to make contact, not to avoid it, so he continued approaching them, neither hurrying his pace nor slowing it.

One of the Fireflies said something to him. He couldn't understand a word.

"Greetings, my brothers," replied Lennox in the Brakkanan dialect. "May I share your shade?"

"You are welcome," said another, replying in the same dialect. "Where is your *kadeko*?"

Kadeko? *What the hell is a* kadeko?

Lennox's mind raced through the possibilities and decided it had to be his mount, though that was not the Brakkanan word for it.

"It broke a leg earlier today."

Do I add that I had to destroy it? Should I be lugging twenty pounds of kadeko *chops over my shoulder?*

"Have you come far afoot?"

How far have I walked? Twelve miles? Fifteen? Better double it, just so they don't go looking for the damned kadeko.

Finally Lennox turned and indicated an outcropping about twenty-five miles away. "I came from there," he said.

"And where are you going?"

"Brakkanan."

"You are *from* Brakkanan?"

"Yes."

Of course I am. Why else would I be speaking it?

"I thought I detected the hint of an accent," said the Firefly. "I was obviously mistaken."

"And where are you three headed?"

"First Borgannan, then Brakkanan. We trade *porst* for *ragush.*"

Porst. That was the spider-silk used on the more exotic formal fabrics. But *ragush*? He'd never heard the word before.

"May I join you?" asked Lennox.

"We have no *kadeko* to spare."

"I will walk."

"You will not be able to keep up."

"At least I will keep you in sight," said Lennox. "I do not wish to travel alone in unfriendly territory."

"The entire desert is unfriendly to solitary travelers."

"That is what I meant, of course," said Lennox.

The three Fireflies consulted among themselves for a moment, then gave him permission to accompany them as best he could. It was only then that they introduced themselves. Their names were Jamarsh, Neshbidan, and Sumriche, and they were from the distant city-state of Talbedon.

"And I am Dromesche," replied Lennox, borrowing the name of the Firefly with whom he had shared the prison cell.

"Are you a trader, too?" asked Jamarsh.

I'd better not be. I don't know the names for half of what gets traded on this world.

"No."

"A warrior, then?"

A mystic, out communing with the spirits, would be better, but I don't know enough about the religion. I'd better take what you give me.

Lennox nodded. "A warrior."

"Where are your weapons?"

You can see my sword and dagger. What else does a warrior carry with him?

"I left them behind with my *kadeko*; they were too burdensome to carry. I will replace them when we reach Borgannan."

"It is foolhardy to travel alone so poorly armed. What if we were *raboni* or *sevensali*?"

Raboni, raboni . . . he'd heard it before. What did it mean? Ah, yes—the nomadic thieves of the desert. *Sevensali?* He didn't recognize it, but it had to be something similar.

"I would have explained that I came in peace."

"The *raboni* do not accept such explanations."

What would a warrior say next?

"Then I would have killed you."

"With only a sword and a dagger?" asked Sumriche.

"That is correct," said Lennox.

"You sound very confident."

"I have survived all my battles. That is cause for confidence in any warrior."

Somebody please change the subject. I'm getting in deeper and deeper.

The three Fireflies went into another huddle. When it broke up, it was Jamarsh who spoke again.

"We will rearrange the burdens, and let you ride one of our *kadekos.*"

A self-assured warrior is a handy thing to have on a world like this, isn't it? Lennox was glad his mouth could no longer form a smile, for he would have had considerable difficulty repressing it.

Neshbidan stared at Lennox. "Have you eaten?" he asked at last.

"Not recently," said Lennox, who had a three-day supply of dried meat in one of his robe's pouches, but wanted to keep it for an emergency.

Neshbidan reached into a pouch and tossed something to him. It looked like a very old, very wrinkled pear. He looked at it for a moment, and then, aware that they were staring at him, bit into it. There wasn't much flavor, but he dutifully chewed and swallowed it, then took another bite. This time it tasted a bit better, and by the time he had finished it he found that he rather liked it.

"We have rested the *kadekos* long enough," announced Jamarsh when Lennox had finished. "We can make it more than halfway to the next oasis by sunset."

Jamarsh indicated which *kadeko* would be Lennox's, and the three Fireflies quickly rearranged their animals' burdens. They had twelve *kadekos* in all, but only the riding animals bore any form of harness. Lennox watched the others mount their beasts, then did the same, and tried to hold the single strap of the halter exactly as they did. Neshbidan immediately took up a position at the rear, and the other two Fireflies indicated that Lennox was to ride at the front with them.

As they began riding, the eight burdened *kadekos* fell in step behind them, matching their pace.

"We will have to find a secure place to spend the night," said Jamarsh. "This part of the desert is filled with *raboni*."

"Why don't we just keep riding?" suggested Lennox, wondering why they didn't lay up in the heat of the day and travel by night, when they would be harder to spot.

"You are either the bravest or craziest warrior I have ever met," replied Jamarsh.

"As you wish," said Lennox. "I'm just a passenger."

"Are you really willing to ride among them at night?" asked Sumriche curiously.

"They are just bandits."

"We are brave *zhandi*"—their name for their species—"but even *we* do not tempt the *raboni*."

"I have seen Men go out among them with no fear," said Lennox, who had been waiting for an opportunity to work his race into the conversation.

"That is because Men are ignorant," said Sumriche. "I have been told they cannot even see at night."

Oh, shit! No wonder they won't ride through raboni *territory at night. Fireflies can see in the dark! And even if I didn't remember that, I should have remembered that we glow in the dark. Watch yourself, Lennox, or you're dead meat on your first day here.*

"They have superior weapons, though," said Lennox at last.

"I have heard that, but I have seen no proof of it," said Jamarsh.

"I have," offered Lennox. "We could learn from them."

"Were you at Brakkanan when they attacked it?" asked Sumriche.

"Yes."

"Is it true that a Man had actually thought he could disguise himself and approach the pyramid?"

"It is true," said Lennox.

Sumriche snorted contemptuously. "That just goes to prove we have nothing to learn from them."

"I don't know," said Lennox. "We have nothing they want, but they have something *we* want: their weapons. I have occasionally thought it would be advantageous to reach an accommodation with them."

"That borders on blasphemy," said Jamarsh harshly. "The *zhandi* are God's Chosen People. We do not reach accommodations with lesser beings."

Lennox decided to let the subject drop. These three traders were not, after all, the people he had to convince. Besides, he'd made enough blunders already; the sooner he reached Borgannan and left their company, the better. He would wait until he understood them better before discussing Men again.

They came to a series of rocky outcroppings just before twilight, and decided to camp for the night. The *kadekos* were tethered, and each of the three Fireflies set up lean-tos to protect them from the blowing sand. None was offered to Lennox, and he didn't request one.

Neshbidan pulled a gourd of water out of his saddle, took two swallows, and replaced it. Jamarsh and Sumriche followed suit. Again, no one offered water to Lennox. He didn't want anyone to see his canteen, since he didn't know if it was the type a warrior would use, so he waited until they were asleep and then took a few sips, surprised that he wasn't more thirsty.

He hadn't become adept at urinating yet—it squirted out behind him, like a cat's—so he also removed his robes and tended to his bodily functions. He found that he was hungry—he might not be interested in human food anymore, but he still had a body to fuel. He didn't want to use his secret supply of dried meat; there was no telling when he might find himself alone again. He briefly considered taking some more of the fruit from Neshbidan's saddlebags. But if he were seen, they would think he was a thief, and his bravado—with which he had hoped to avoid any conflicts—would do him no good.

Still, the more he tried to put the thought of food out of his mind, the hungrier he became. He was just on the verge of withdrawing a piece of meat when he saw another of the scarablike insects crawling on a rock a few feet away from him. This time he wasted no time in killing it, and, reminding himself that he was no longer human and that this disgusting thing in his hands actually tasted good, he closed his eyes and bit into it, and had totally consumed it in a matter of seconds.

He caught four more in the next half hour, then

walked over to a lone tree and sampled its flowers and leaves. He knew what Fireflies ate, of course—he'd observed one at very close quarters while in jail, and had looked into quite a few kitchens in Brakkanan. But the meat and fruit that formed their staple diet were nowhere to be found, and so he ate almost half a pound of prickly blossoms and leathery leaves with the fervent hope that they weren't harmful to his new body.

He awoke feeling mildly nauseated, but it passed within a few minutes, and he knew that if he used up his secret cache of meat he could live off the desert landscape for at least a few days. Neshbidan, who seemed to be in charge of the food, tossed him another dried fruit; this time he pretended to eat it but managed to hide it in a pouch on the inside of his robe; the thought of eating anything just now made him queasy again. They all had their customary two swallows of water, and then the three Fireflies mounted up. Lennox followed suit, and a moment later was once again riding across the sun-baked desert.

Even with his new metabolism, he soon began feeling uncomfortable in the desert heat. Either it was hotter than yesterday, which seemed doubtful, or else he needed more fluids than he seemed to crave. There was no way to take a surreptitious drink from his canteen, so he bore the discomfort in silence and hoped it wouldn't get much worse.

Jamarsh and Sumriche engaged in occasional conversations. Rather than trying to participate, Lennox listened carefully and tried to figure out the meanings of those terms he didn't know. It was easier than the previous day, for he wasn't trying to reply while thinking one sentence ahead. The three Fireflies had been on the trail for almost four months, and it would be another five before they would return to their homes. There had been a fourth member of the caravan, but he had died in a duel a month ago. Lennox wanted to ask if the duel had been with one of his partners, or with someone else, and what they felt was worth fighting to the death over, but he couldn't find a way to couch his questions without exposing his ignorance.

In midmorning they stopped and dismounted, and Lennox did likewise. They turned to the northwest, raised their hands above their heads, and stood motionless for a long moment, then climbed back on their *kadekos* and resumed their journey. Lennox assumed they had been praying, but none of them had uttered a word and he didn't dare ask, since he, too, had stood with his hands raised. *Just in case we get separated or I do have to kill you, it would be helpful if you were praying to the pyramid, so I'll know what direction to go.*

He couldn't tell how they navigated across the desert, but they altered course twice to find oases. They allowed the *kadekos* to drink long and deep at the first one—and Lennox himself managed to sneak some water from his canteen and refill it when his companions went off in opposite directions, presumably to tend to their bodily functions in private. They all sat in the shade when they came to the second one shortly after midday, neither the Fireflies nor their mounts evincing any desire to drink again.

Lennox noticed a quick motion out of the corner of his eye and turned toward it. For an instant nothing happened, but then he saw it again and darted his hand into the sand where he had seen it. His fingers came into contact with something that squirmed and tried to get loose, and, tightening his grip, he pulled a fat succulent eyeless worm, perhaps two feet long, out of the ground. It turned and tried to rake its hairy tongue against his hand. He assumed that the tongue was dangerous if not deadly, and quickly shifted his grip so that he held it just behind its head.

My God, this body is quick! No human could have moved fast enough to catch this thing.

"Excellent, Dromesche!" said Neshbidan. "We will eat well tonight."

He pulled out a knife, walked over, and decapitated the worm. The body continued to squirm as in life, and Lennox was momentarily at a loss as to what to do with it. If he tossed it onto the ground, it might very well burrow into the sand in its thrashing and be lost to him; if he continued to hold it as it spurted bodily fluids, he might again expose his ignorance, in case it was worthless without them.

He quickly considered his options and hit upon a solution.

"It is my gift to you," he said, tossing the writhing body to Neshbidan.

The Firefly caught the worm and instantly pinched the flesh together just behind where he had beheaded it. The flow of fluids immediately stopped.

"I accept your gracious gift," he said, bowing low.

"You came very close to losing your hand," noted Jamarsh. "Very few *zhandi* would attempt to catch a blindworm without a weapon."

"It is only a blindworm," said Lennox with a shrug,

making a mental note never again to reach his hand into the sand after something he could not see.

"Like I said yesterday," replied Jamarsh. "Brave or crazy."

"He will soon have a chance to prove which," said Sumriche, peering out across the desert.

"What do you mean?" asked Lennox, with an uneasy feeling in the pit of his stomach.

Sumriche pointed to the horizon, where a number of riders had just appeared.

"*Raboni,*" he said.

NINE

❧❧❧❧❧❧❧❧❧❧❧❧❧❧

Wonderful, thought Lennox wryly. *If I confront these bandits, they'll kill me—and if I don't, and we survive it, my own companions will kill me. Not without some justification, either—I told them I was a warrior. That's why they let me ride with them.*

He had an instinct to shield his eyes from the sun with his hand and watch the *raboni* approach, but caught himself just in time. His new eyes didn't *need* shielding, and he had never seen a Firefly make the gesture.

"There is no sense fleeing," said Jamarsh. "They are between us and Borgannan. If we go back the way we came, they will catch us sooner or later. Perhaps this way they will merely rob us and let us live."

"I will begin unloading the *kadekos* so they will know we do not plan to oppose them," said Neshbidan.

"Don't," said Lennox.

"Why not?"

"They're going to take your goods anyway. Why abase yourselves?"

"So that they will not take our lives."

"Perhaps there is a third way," said Lennox. "I will speak to them."

"Speaking will do no good. They are *raboni.*"

"If they're going to rob you anyway, you've nothing to lose. *You* don't have to speak or appear antagonistic. Just don't contradict anything I say to them."

"What will you say?" asked Sumriche.

Don't rush me. I'm working on it.

"Whatever it is, I want the three of you to keep quiet. If you don't, I will kill you before they can kill me."

Think hard, Lennox. You were imprisoned with one. You've spoken to several others. The one thing they have in common is that every last one of them is grim and serious. You've never heard one tell a joke, or even comprehend one. You've never heard one lie. Is it just vaguely possible they are strangers to deceit, whether humorous or serious?

He considered the possibility. *They've had no intercourse with Man, so where would they have learned it?*

The closest of the *raboni* was now within fifty yards.

It's crazy. But on the other hand, if I don't think of something, one side or the other is going to cut me to pieces. Just remember to look confident, to speak with authority, and hope that they've never seen a bluff before.

"Greetings, my brothers," said Lennox as the *raboni* spread out to surround them. "You were wise to seek me out."

The Firefly who seemed to be the leader of the group almost did a double take.

"Explain yourself," he said in gruff, guttural tones.

"I bear you no ill will, and am willing to place you under my protection until we reach Borgannan."

The Firefly frowned. "What foolishness is this?"

"I am the advance scout for a party of three hundred warriors who are traveling to Borgannan," continued Lennox. "I have offered these traders my protection. I am happy to do the same for you."

"You are but four *zhandi*," said the Firefly. "We need no protection from you."

"That is true," said Lennox. "But you need protection from those who follow me."

The Firefly stared long and hard at him. "What is to stop us from robbing and slaying you before your warriors arrive?"

"Common sense," answered Lennox. "I will surely kill at least one of you, probably many, and they will know from the corpses who was responsible."

"We can pick up the bodies and ride away with them."

Well, at least you believe I can kill some of you. Let's hope that's a step in the right direction.

"Why spill blood needlessly?" replied Lennox.

"What kind of warrior's code is *that*?" demanded the Firefly contemptuously.

You did it again, Lennox. Try to remember: these are not nice guys; spilling blood is their way of life. Better double-talk your way out of this, fast.

"It is the code of a warrior who disdains waste," said Lennox. "I have already offered you my protection.

What purpose would be served by killing those I have agreed to protect?''

''You speak unlike any warrior I have ever met,'' said the Firefly contemptuously. ''If all three hundred are like you, we shall destroy them.''

''Others have thought so,'' said Lennox with no show of concern.

''I am not others.''

The Firefly turned and surveyed his twenty armed comrades.

Jesus! He's going to do it! He's going to give the kill order. Think of something—anything!

''You are a fool,'' said Lennox. ''You cannot even kill me, and yet you brag about slaughtering three hundred warriors.''

The Firefly dismounted. ''We shall see whether I can kill you or not.''

''I will strike a bargain with you,'' said Lennox. ''If you can kill me in personal combat, our goods are yours, and my companions will swear fealty to you. But if you cannot, then you will accept my protection, and will accompany us to Borgannan as brothers.''

''Done!'' cried the Firefly.

And let's hope you've never seen a boxing or karate match.

''Wait!'' said Lennox, holding up a hand. The Firefly froze, and Lennox removed his robe and his weapons. ''To prove that I need no weapons to defeat a *raboni*,'' he explained. *Also, because I'm still not used to that damned robe, and I don't want to trip over it at the wrong time.*

"You think to defeat me without a sword or a dagger?" said the Firefly, surprised.

I was rather hoping you might respond in kind.

"I only use weapons when I need them."

"As you wish," said the Firefly, drawing its long, hook-ended sword and approaching him.

Calmly, calmly. Remember that this body can't do all the things your old one could.

Lennox held his arms away from his body and circled to the left, looking for an opening. The Firefly, puzzled and perhaps apprehensive by his disdain for weapons, approached him cautiously. Suddenly the blade shot out and tore a chunk of flesh from Lennox's left arm. He wondered if his face was capable of reflecting the pain he felt.

The Firefly approached again, more confidently this time.

Do something quick, Lennox. If he reaches you again, you're dead meat.

Lennox feinted to his right, then launched a spinning kick that landed on the Firefly's knee. He felt bone and cartilage crunch beneath his foot, and the Firefly collapsed to the ground. Lennox followed up his advantage, stepping forward and kicking the sword out of the Firefly's hand.

He picked up the weapon and pointed it toward the Firefly.

Do Fireflies offer mercy to defeated opponents? Will I be giving myself away if I do? Damn you, Nora Wallace! You sent me here too soon! There's still too much I don't know.

Torn by indecision, he stood motionless before the

Firefly, who finally raised his hand in a brief gesture. The tension immediately left the other *raboni* and Lennox's three companions, and he concluded that his opponent had yielded. Still, he remained as he was, waiting for a more certain sign.

"We accept your protection," said the Firefly at last, and finally Lennox tossed the sword away.

Then he turned to the *raboni*. "Some of you help tend to his leg and try to make him comfortable."

"Why?" asked one of them. "You have crippled him. He will never walk again. Better to kill him now."

Such compassion for a defeated comrade.

"He can ride," said Lennox. "I have promised *all* of you my protection. That includes him." Suddenly a thought occurred to him. "And he can be made to walk again with as sure a stride as he possessed this morning."

"That is impossible."

"It is impossible for us," answered Lennox. "But not for Men. Their medicine can restore or replace broken limbs."

"How do you know this?" demanded another *raboni*.

"My warriors have spied on them," said Lennox. "At first we thought to make war on them, but then, as we discovered how many things we had to learn from them, we decided it might be better to allow them to live among us."

"We are the Chosen People. That is blasphemy."

Lennox pointed to the fallen Firefly. "Ask *him* if he thinks it is blasphemous to walk without pain, without even a limp."

"I will hear no more of this," said the protesting *raboni,* turning away and walking to his *kadeko.*

"And you?" asked Lennox of his opponent.

"If they can make me whole again," grated the Firefly, "and a warrior such as yourself is willing to treat with them, I will at least listen to you."

"That is all I ask," said Lennox.

All right, it's a small triumph, but a triumph nonetheless. I just hope I don't have to put my life on the line every time I want to convince one of you that Men are not your enemies.

TEN

❦❦❦❦❦❦❦❦❦❦❦❦❦❦

The crippled *raboni*'s name was Borleshan, and since he seemed the most reasonable of them, Lennox chose to ride beside him. Far from being bitter about his defeat, Borleshan overcame his obvious pain long enough to ask numerous questions about Lennox's method of fighting, and Lennox lost no time explaining that he had learned it by spying upon Men.

"I am puzzled," announced Borleshan at last.

"About what?"

"About Men," answered the Firefly. "If they have such fighting abilities, and such medical skills, and can traverse the stars at will, why have they not simply marched in and conquered us?"

"Perhaps they have no desire to do so," suggested Lennox.

"Then why are they here at all?"

"I have heard that they wish to trade with us."

"What do they possess that we could possibly want?" asked another *raboni* contemptuously.

"Knowledge."

Borleshan considered Lennox's answer for a moment. "And what would we trade for it?"

Lennox shrugged. "I do not know," he said. "Perhaps we should ask them."

"I have no objection," said Borleshan. "But, of course, it is not up to me."

Lennox wanted to know who it *was* up to, but didn't dare display his ignorance by asking. "Perhaps when they fix your leg, we can find out," he suggested at last.

"You plan to ride right into their camp?" asked a *raboni.* "They will kill us all!"

"I doubt it," said Lennox, with what he hoped was an air of certainty. "This is *our* world. If they wish to be allowed to stay here, even in an outpost, they will not kill us."

"They have no respect for us," said Borleshan. "Have you not heard that one of them actually went to the pyramid?"

News sure does get around.

"We killed him, of course?" said Lennox.

"Chomanche himself was about to administer the death blow, when other Men came to his rescue. My understanding is that we killed three of them, and they killed seven of us."

Chomanche "himself"? God, I hope he's not the one I eventually have to convince.

"Perhaps the Man had some reason to be there," suggested Lennox.

"We have warned Men to stay away from Brakka-nan, and especially from the pyramid," said Borleshan firmly. "He knew the consequences of his actions."

"I am told that Men have a pervasive curiosity," said Lennox. "Were you never so curious about anything that you ignored advice or warnings?"

"Never," said Borleshan, eyeing him strangely. "But your question arouses my curiosity."

"I am simply trying to think the way the Man thought," said Lennox hastily, as several of the *raboni* turned to stare at him. "It is good practice, since I will soon be asking their doctors to fix your leg." They seemed to accept that, so he continued: "Perhaps, since Men trade in knowledge, he was simply trying to acquire more goods, so to speak."

"He could not trade it to *us*," said Borleshan. "That means he would trade it to someone else."

"That is true," agreed Lennox. "But consider the consequences."

"What consequences?" said another *raboni*. "The only consequence is that the Man must die."

"Since we are the Chosen People, and our faith is the only true faith, perhaps letting other races learn about it is a good idea."

Borleshan stared at him for a long moment. "You are a most unusual *zhandi*, Dromesche," he said. "You are a warrior, but you do not kill. You speak blasphemy, and yet it possesses a certain logic."

"Their weapons are more powerful than ours," responded Lennox. "Therefore, as a warrior I know that if we are ever to fight against them, we must become more clever than they are. And the only way to become more clever than your enemy is to study him until you know him as well as he knows himself.''

"I say kill them all," said a *raboni,* placing his hand to the hilt of his sword.

"*You* kill them all," said Lennox. "We will applaud your victory."

The *raboni* glared at him but made no reply.

They rode in silence for the next hour, Borleshan because of his pain, Lennox because he saw no need to be killed as a heretic before he reached Brakkanan. Then, when Lennox saw that Borleshan was swaying in the saddle as if he might momentarily pass out, he called a halt as they reached the shade of a huge rocky outcrop. When all the Fireflies had dismounted, he announced that his destination was the human outpost south of Brakkanan.

"None of you have to come with us," he said. "But I have given Borleshan my word that Men can make him whole again, and I intend to keep it."

"They will kill you both," said one of the *raboni.*

"If you are afraid to come with us, then go your own way," said Lennox.

"I will do so now," said the *raboni,* mounting his *kadeko* The other *raboni* all followed suit.

"But know that once you leave, you are no longer under my protection," continued Lennox. "If my warriors find you, they will kill you."

"Better to die with a sword in my hand, looking into my enemy's eyes, than to be killed at a great distance by the weapons of Men," answered the *raboni.*

"As you wish," said Lennox. "But you will leave the three traders unharmed, or I will seek each of you out and kill you. I have seen your faces. I know who you are.''

"They have safe passage," said Borleshan. He turned to his companions. "I have given the word of a *raboni*. You must honor it.''

The *raboni* who had spoken first reluctantly nodded his agreement, then wheeled his mount and trotted off across the desert, followed by his comrades.

Lennox turned to the three traders. "I know you have business in Borgannan," he said. "You have helped a lone wayfarer, and I hope I have repaid you for your generosity. You need not accompany us to the human outpost. Your safety is guaranteed.''

"Thank you, Dromesche," said Jamarsh. "Perhaps we shall meet again in Brakkanan.''

"It's possible," said Lennox. "Go now. Borleshan requires more rest.''

Each of the three bowed to him, and Neshbidan went to his saddle and brought him a bag filled with dried fruit. Then they, too, mounted up and left.

Lennox glanced at Borleshan's knee, which had swollen to twice its normal size.

"It looks bad," he said, indicating the knee.

"I have not complained," said the Firefly stoically.

Remember: practicality, not compassion.

"I know. But it is obvious that you are in pain. Discomfort. The sooner we get you to the outpost, the sooner you will once again be able to ride and fight efficiently.''

"There's no rush," said Borleshan. "The pain is too great for them to work on my knee, even if they agree to. It could be weeks before it subsides.''

"They will give you something to alleviate the pain before they go to work."

Borleshan seemed surprised. "Can they do that?"

"So I have been told."

"You make them sound like gods," said Borleshan.

Am I overdoing it? Or should *I make them sound like gods?*

"Their knowledge is not magical," replied Lennox. "It is merely different from ours."

He helped Borleshan onto his *kadeko* an hour later, and the two proceeded at a leisurely pace toward the human outpost. Lennox had hoped to learn something of Brakkanan and the pyramid, but the Firefly was in no mood to talk, and he elected not to pursue the subject.

The journey was uneventful—they encountered no traders, no warriors, and no *raboni*—and on the third afternoon they reached an oasis that was within four miles of the human outpost. Lennox helped Borleshan dismount, tethered the Firefly's *kadeko,* and brought the wounded *raboni* some water to drink.

"I'm going to go on to the outpost," said Lennox, when Borleshan was comfortably settled, "and explain the situation. I should be back before morning."

"If you are not, I will know that you are dead, and I will attempt to rejoin my comrades," said Borleshan.

"Wait until tomorrow nightfall," said Lennox. "I don't know how many medics they have. It may take a full day before one is free to come back here with me."

"A full day?" repeated Borleshan. "I do not like it."

"You have trusted me this far," said Lennox. "Trust me a little farther."

Borleshan considered the request, then nodded his assent, and Lennox mounted his *kadeko*.

"You have defeated me in battle, yet you have spared my life," he said as Lennox began riding off. "If they kill you, know that you will be avenged."

If they kill me, I hope to hell you do *avenge me.*

ELEVEN

Laennox stood patiently at the gate to the fortress as first one human soldier, then more, noticed him and trained their weapons on him. Finally the gate slid back and an officer emerged and approached him.

"May I see Colonel Mbaka, please?" said Lennox, finding that he had great difficulty pronouncing the words.

"Who are you?" demanded the officer.

"You're going to have a hard time believing this," said Lennox, "but my name is Xavier William Lennox, and I am a Man."

" 'Hard' would be an understatement," replied the officer. "What do you want and where did you learn our language?"

"Colonel Mbaka is aware of my situation," said Lennox. "If you will just take me to him . . ."

"Lieutenant Colonel Mbaka is out on a reconnaissance mission, unless you Fireflies have killed him," replied the officer. "How did you know his name?"

"I told you. I am Xavier William Lennox, and I am here on a mission for the Department of Alien Affairs."

"Listen to me, Firefly," snapped the officer. "It's one hundred and twenty-seven degrees out, and I've got better things to do with my time than let you keep telling me you're a Man. I'm asking you again: what is your business here?"

"A friend of mine has injured his leg," said Lennox. "I want our medics to fix it."

"*Our* medics?" repeated the officer.

"That's right."

The officer snapped his fingers. "Just like that?"

"Look," said Lennox, "I know this is difficult for you to believe, but I am a surgically altered human being, here on a secret diplomatic mission."

"Follow me," said the officer, leading him into the fortress. Lennox entered the building and felt immediate discomfort as the cooled air hit him.

"I need a robe or a blanket of some kind," he announced. "During the surgery my metabolism was altered. I feel like I'm walking around naked on a polar planet."

"Right in there," said the officer, pointing to a room off to his left.

Lennox entered the room, found nothing in it, and turned back to the officer. Suddenly he was facing three armed men. The officer touched a button on the outside of the wall, and a translucent force field hummed into existence.

"All right," said the officer. "Now suppose you tell us who you *really* are, and how you learned to speak Terran."

"I told you. My name is Xavier William Lennox. I am a Man, born on Earth, current residence Athena II. I have been surgically altered to resemble a Firefly."

"Where did you hear of Athena II?"

"I *live* there, goddamnit!"

"Sure you do." The officer smiled. "And of course you're Lennox. He's the only Man that the Fireflies know by name."

"Will you just contact Colonel Mbaka? He can confirm what I'm saying."

"How do you happen to know Mbaka's name?"

"It was given to me by Nora Wallace of the Department of Alien Affairs."

"Never heard of her," said the officer.

"There's no reason why you should have. Her contact here was Colonel Mbaka."

"That's awfully convenient, isn't it? I mean, someone we never heard of has as her only contact an officer that you know is away from the outpost? And you yourself are the one Man whose name is known to the Fireflies?" He shook his head in mock regret. "I was really hoping you savages would be smarter than this."

"When is Mbaka due back?"

"None of your business."

"It's all of our business," said Lennox. "He'll confirm my identity."

"Then just make yourself at home and wait."

"Listen to me, damn it! There's a Firefly suffering

out in the desert—a Firefly who's willing to believe that it's better to talk to Men than make war against them.''

''I thought that was *you*,'' said the officer sardonically.

''He's not going to wait for more than a day. Let him go and we'll have blown a beautiful opportunity.''

''An opportunity for what? To let a couple of Fireflies on a suicide mission come in here and destroy our fortress?''

''I'm unarmed. You know that.''

''All I know is that I've got a prisoner who thought he could bluff his way in with the most ridiculous story I've ever heard,'' said the officer. He turned to leave. ''I'll talk to you when you're ready to tell the truth.''

Lennox grabbed his arm. ''I *am* telling the truth, goddamnit!''

The officer responded with the quickness of a cat, knocking him back into a wall.

''Don't ever touch me again, Firefly!'' he snapped.

Lennox cleared his head and forced himself to respond in a calm voice. ''Do you have anyone on your staff who's been posted here for more than eight months?''

''Why?''

''Because I was here eight months ago. I can recall incidents that happened then, incidents only a Man who was here at the time could know, and they'll know I'm telling the truth.''

''Nice try,'' said the officer. ''But I was there when we rescued Lennox. There wasn't a hell of a lot of him left. Who knows what you bastards got out of him before we arrived?'' He paused and stared at Lennox.

"You want to play games? Okay. How many of us were in the rescue party?"

"I don't know."

"How many of us carried you back to the vehicle that brought you here?"

"I was unconscious," said Lennox. "You know that."

"You weren't unconscious when the doc went to work on you," said the officer. "What was his name?"

"I don't know."

The officer smiled. "You don't know the name of the man who saved your life?"

"I was in a state of shock!" snapped Lennox in frustration. "I don't remember anything after they impaled me to the ground."

"How very convenient," said the officer. "I'm going to give you an hour to reconsider your story. Then we'll talk."

He left, followed by the three guards, and Lennox found himself alone in his cell. There was no mattress, no blanket, no water outlet, no toilet . . . just four walls, a floor, a ceiling, and a force field.

He walked to a corner, gently lowered himself to the floor, and leaned back against the walls. Why the hell did he have to show up here on a day when Mbaka was gone? He'd risked his life to get Borleshan to listen to him and agree to come here. It was the first small breakthrough, and these idiots were going to piss it away.

Lennox watched soldiers marching past in the corridor, heard voices giving commands, and began feeling very sorry for himself. Then he thought of Borleshan, lying in the desert with a knee the size of a grapefruit, and anger replaced self-pity. How had he managed to get into this ridiculous situation in the first place?

Eventually the officer returned. The force field blinked off long enough for him to enter the room, then hummed to life again. Two armed guards stood at the ready just beyond the doorway, their laser weapons trained on Lennox.

"Is there any part of your story you would like to reconsider?" he asked.

"I realize how crazy it must sound," said Lennox, "but it's all true. If you doubt me, why not ask me questions only a Man would know?"

"I did—and you didn't know them."

"I told you: I was in shock from pain and loss of blood. Ask me something else. Ask me about the layout of the fortress."

"Now how the hell did you find out about *that*?"

"I lived here for five months."

"Jesus—you guys really put that poor bastard through the wringer, didn't you? I'm surprised he even knew his name when you were done with him."

"It was my own fault. I ignored their warnings and entered a forbidden area."

"Don't give me your justifications," said the officer. "He was a Man and you cut him to ribbons. That's all I have to know."

"I don't hold it against them," said Lennox. "Why should you?"

"I'm getting a little tired of this act," said the officer. "It's ludicrous." He leaned forward until his face was just inches away from Lennox's. "Now I'm asking you politely for the last time: who are you and what are you doing here?''

''I am Xavier William Lennox, and I am seeking medical help for a Firefly friend.''

The officer's hand shot out and slapped Lennox hard across the face.

''Again,'' he said. ''Who are you and why are you here?''

''It doesn't make any difference whether I'm Lennox or a Firefly,'' said Lennox, tasting blood on his lip. ''You're supposed to be befriending Fireflies, not going to war with them. I have a friend in need of medical help.''

Another slap.

''Befriending Fireflies is another union,'' said the officer. ''My job is the security of the outpost. Who are you?''

''Xavier William Lennox.''

This time it was a fist, and Lennox fought to remain conscious.

''I've got all day,'' said the officer. ''Who are you?''

''Dromesche.''

''That's better,'' said the officer. ''Now, why are you here?''

''I have a friend who requires medical treatment.''

''How did you learn to speak Terran?''

''It's my native tongue.''

Another slap.

''How did you learn to speak Terran?''

''I learned it from Xavier William Lennox.''

''When?''

Lennox was still trying to come up with an answer

that would avoid another blow when the officer's fist thudded into his belly. He doubled over, gasping for breath.

"You're not being very smart," said the officer. "This hurts you a lot more than it hurts me."

"Tell your men to put away their weapons and we'll see who hurts who the most!" grated Lennox.

"You'd like that, wouldn't you?" said the officer. He wrapped his fingers around Lennox's jaw and pulled his head up. "When did Lennox teach you Terran?"

"In Brakkanan."

A heavy blow to the head.

"Lennox was only in Brakkanan for one day. You couldn't have learned it that fast. When did he teach you?"

"I give up," said Lennox wearily. "You tell me."

"I don't like your attitude," said the officer. "You come in here with the stupidest story I've ever heard, you answer every question with a lie . . . no, I don't like your attitude at all. In fact, I can't think of a single thing I *do* like about you."

"The feeling is mutual."

"Now that I think about it, I can't see any reason why I shouldn't kill you right here and now."

"*I* can," said Lennox.

"Then perhaps you'd like to share it with me while you have time."

"The corridor outside this room leads past the mess hall and the recreation room and ends at the commanding officer's quarters. Inside the compound, against the northeast wall, is the arsenal. The infirmary is right next to the subspace transmitting station."

The officer stared at him. "How do you know all that?"

"I know it because I'm Xavier William Lennox, but since you don't want to believe that, you're going to have to believe that I'm a Firefly, and that if I know it, my comrades know it—and you're going to have to keep me alive long enough to find out how much more I know and who I've told."

"I'll find out, never fear," said the officer, sounding just a little less sure of himself.

"In the meantime," continued Lennox, "I advise you not to physically abuse me, because when Mbaka returns he's going to have your hide if I suffer any permanent damage."

"Are you giving me orders?" demanded the officer.

"No," replied Lennox. "Just a suggestion. If I live long enough, I expect you to thank me for it."

The officer backed away two steps and stared uncertainly at Lennox.

"All right," he said at last. "Colonel Mbaka is due back tomorrow. Let *him* decide what to do with you."

He walked to the doorway and waited for the force field to shut down, then reactivated it when he was in the hall.

"I'd like a blanket and a cot," said Lennox.

The officer turned to one of the guards. "See that he gets them."

"And some water."

The officer nodded. "And water."

"Thank you."

"Where's your friend—the one who needs treatment?"

"In the desert," replied Lennox.

"Give me his location and we'll bring him in."

"I thought you didn't believe anything I said."

"We'll bring him in as a prisoner and give him any medical assistance he needs. Lieutenant Colonel Mbaka can decide what to do with him."

"We'll wait until tomorrow," said Lennox. "I'll have to accompany you. If he doesn't see me, he'll either kill you or try to escape."

"Why?" demanded the officer sharply. "I thought he was more interested in talking than fighting."

"He doesn't know you like I do," said Lennox with what he hoped was a sardonic smile.

TWELVE

⸙⸘ ⸙⸘ ⸙⸘ ⸙⸘ ⸙⸘ ⸙⸘ ⸙⸘

Thanks to his new, improved senses, Lennox was wide awake when the footsteps came to a halt outside his cell. He sat up alertly and looked out into the corridor. A moment later the force field was deactivated, and a small black man stepped through the doorway.

"Mister Lennox?"

"Yes," said Lennox, getting awkwardly to his feet. "Are you Colonel Mbaka?"

"Yes. I apologize for the treatment you have received at our hands. Those responsible for it have already been punished."

"Good."

Mbaka arched an eyebrow. "That's an interesting response," he said.

"It is?"

The colonel nodded. "I had rather expected you to

say something to the effect that they were just doing their duty and that you understood their position.''

"Fuck 'em," said Lennox.

"Come, come, Mister Lennox. You must admit your story sounds unbelievable.''

"What's the difference?" Lennox shot back. "If that's the way you treat unarmed Fireflies, it's no wonder they want you off the planet.''

The colonel considered it, then nodded. "A point well taken." He paused. "Won't you accompany me to my office? We have things to discuss.''

"You bet we do," said Lennox, promptly falling into step behind him.

As they walked along the corridor and past the mess hall, he was aware of the curious and frequently hostile stares he was receiving from the military men and women seated there. He looked around for the officer who had imprisoned and beaten him, but the man was nowhere to be seen. *Just as well. I can imagine his friends' reactions to seeing him attacked by a Firefly.*

Finally they came to Mbaka's spartanly furnished office. The colonel sat down behind a desk, and gestured to Lennox to take a chair facing him.

"I'd rather stand," said Lennox. "Human furniture is very uncomfortable for my new body.''

"As you wish," said Mbaka. "Can I offer you anything, Mister Lennox? A drink, perhaps?''

Lennox shook his head. "I'm afraid not. My metabolism can't handle it.''

"All right," said Mbaka with a shrug. "I have been instructed to help you in any way I can—but no one has told me exactly *why* you're on Medina. If it's not classified, I'd like to be briefed."

"That's simple enough," answered Lennox. "I've been given six months to get the Fireflies to allow us to set up mining operations in the desert outside Brakkanan. No one has told me what will happen if I fail, but I'll bet there won't be any Fireflies left to deal with two years from now."

"That isn't your concern," said Mbaka. "You're not in the military or the diplomatic corps, and I know you're not a geologist. Why were *you* chosen?"

"Because I know more about the Fireflies than any other Man, and I can speak one of their dialects—the one that's used in Brakkanan."

Mbaka surveyed the creature standing in front of him with open curiosity. "How long did it take them to turn you into . . . *this*?"

"A few months."

"May I ask you a personal question?"

"Go ahead," said Lennox.

"Why did you agree to it?" asked Mbaka.

"It'll sell a lot of books."

Mbaka looked unconvinced. "If you need a physical transformation to sell books, you must not be much of a writer to begin with."

"Also, I don't want to see yet another genocide perpetrated on an innocent race."

"Innocent of what, Mister Lennox?" demanded Mbaka. "Surely not torture or dismemberment." He paused. "Besides, I've read your dossier, and you've done nothing to prevent the extermination of other races."

Why am *I sitting here in an alien body? Is "because I could" a legitimate answer?*

"Did you want to ask a question or did you want to argue?" said Lennox irritably.

Mbaka stared coldly at Lennox. "What exactly do you want from me?"

"There's a Firefly named Borleshan out in the desert a few miles from here. He's in need of immediate medical attention. I want to bring him here."

"What's the matter with him?" asked Mbaka sharply. "Is he contagious?"

"He's got a broken kneecap and almost certainly some serious tendon and ligament damage. I want your best surgeon to put him back together."

"How did it happen?"

"I did it to him."

"And now you want to help him?"

"It's a long story," said Lennox. "But he trusts me, and he's willing to trust you, and that's more than any other Firefly has ever done. It's a foot in the door, and I don't want to let the opportunity pass."

"Has he some official standing in Brakkanan?"

Lennox shook his head. "He's a *raboni*."

"A *raboni?*"

"An outlaw."

Mbaka frowned. "Now I'm thoroughly confused," he said. "You damaged an outlaw's knee, and suddenly you've decided he's an essential contact with a legitimate government?"

"Their society isn't like ours," explained Lennox. "The *raboni* are a respected caste who roam the deserts. They have a strict code of behavior. They don't break the laws within the cities, and they're allowed free passage through them.''

"But how can he possibly help you convince the leaders of Brakkanan to—"

"He can tell any Firefly who will listen to him that not all Men are out to kill them," interrupted Lennox. "You repair his leg and set him loose, and he'll tell the story in every city he travels through." Lennox paused. "I should point out that it will be the first favorable publicity we've gotten since the day we landed."

"How do you know he'll go to Brakkanan at all?"

"I'll take him there."

"You're friends?"

"Not exactly."

"Well, then?"

"Just take my word for it," said Lennox with certainty. "If we fix his leg and I ask him to come to Brakkanan with me, he'll come."

"Well, you're the Firefly expert, so if you say he'll go with you, I'll have to take your word for it." Mbaka paused in thought for a moment, then looked up. "I'll send a party out for him immediately."

"I'll have to accompany it. If he sees your men and I'm not with them, he'll fight or run."

"How can he run on a bad leg?"

"He's got a *kadeko*."

"What's that—one of those animals they ride?"

"Yes."

"All right, Mister Lennox," said Mbaka. "Is there anything else?"

"Yes, there is."

"What?"

"From this moment on," said Lennox, "I want you to open your infirmary to any unarmed Firefly that comes here in need of medical aid."

Mbaka frowned. "How many more have you got hidden out there in the desert?"

"None. But their knowledge of medicine is just about nil. If we are to convince them to deal with us, we have to be able to offer them something they want in exchange for the rights to mine diamonds. Medicine seems more practical and less dangerous than weapons."

"We know very little of Firefly physiology," said Mbaka carefully. "We could make a mistake and convince them we're out to kill them."

"The Department of Alien Affairs can put you in touch with a Doctor Beatrice Ngoni, the surgeon who supervised my metamorphosis. She has dissected a number of Firefly corpses, and can transmit her data to your doctors. As for diseases, you'll just have to do your best, and hope most of them are too weak to make their way here."

"It could take days for us to contact this Doctor Ngoni and have her send us her data via subspace radio."

"It'll be days before you see any Firefly patients," Lennox assured him. "First, Borleshan has to spread the word, and second, they have to get used to the idea that you won't kill them on sight."

"All right. Is there anything else?"

"Just one thing."

"And what is that?" asked Mbaka.

"I don't care if you fix Borleshan's knee or replace it," said Lennox. "I don't care if he walks out on his own leg or a prosthetic one. But he'd damned well better not limp or feel any pain.''

"That's a tall order, Mister Lennox," said Mbaka.

"Considering that you expect to avoid a war and plunder this world of millions of diamonds in exchange for it, I should think it's actually a very simple order.''

"For a writer with delusions of grandeur, perhaps," said Mbaka. "For a medic who's never worked on a Firefly before, not necessarily.''

"I used to be a writer, and someday I will be again," said Lennox. "But right now I'm a Firefly. And if anyone here suggests otherwise to Borleshan, I stand every chance of becoming a dead Firefly.''

"I can't imagine why you're worried about a Firefly that you've already crippled.''

"He has friends who are willing to believe the worst about Men," said Lennox. "Maybe thirty or forty million of them," he added wryly.

THIRTEEN

Two weeks had passed since the reconstructive surgery on Borleshan's knee. Lennox spent most of his time with the Firefly, ostensibly to comfort him, actually to learn more of the language and customs of his race.

"If he were an athlete, I wouldn't let him work out for another two months," the surgeon had told Lennox on the day Borleshan was released. "But I've been told that you can't spare the time. I've been in contact with Doctor Ngoni, and we think the pills I gave him will block most of the pain. But if he stresses the knee, he could damage it again and then the only solution would be a prosthesis."

"I'll make sure he takes the pills," Lennox had said.

"I also don't want him doing anything strenuous. He's got to get plenty of rest."

"I'll see to it."

"I'm told that I can expect to learn a hell of a lot more about Firefly physiology in the coming months, all because of you," said the doctor as Lennox left his office.

"That's right."

"Don't do me any more favors."

Lennox stopped by Borleshan's quarters and accompanied him out the front of the fortress, where their *kadekos* were saddled and waiting.

"How does your knee feel today?" asked Lennox as they headed north toward Brakkanan.

"It hurts until I take one of the small pellets, and then the pain vanishes," answered the Firefly.

"Well, just remember to keep taking them as the doctor instructed you to."

"It occurs to me, Dromesche, that these pellets could be a ploy."

"If you think they don't work, try walking around our camp tomorrow morning before you've taken one," said Lennox.

"You misunderstand," said Borleshan. "I mean that they are a way for the Men to keep us under continual obligation to them. It is true that the human doctor fixed my leg, but it is also true that I cannot function without use of the pellets. I will eventually have to return to the outpost for more of them."

"It is you who do not understand," replied Lennox. "I spoke with the doctor. He had to cut open your leg, repair the kneecap, and reattach many ligaments and tendons. This is a severe insult to your system, and causes extreme pain until you are healed. These pellets mask the pain. It is still there, but you cannot feel it. It will diminish each day, and by the time you run through your supply of pellets, your pain will have vanished and you will no longer need them.''

''How can a pellet mask pain?'' asked Borleshan dubiously.

''I do not know,'' said Lennox. ''I am not a Man. But let us say you receive a wound to your foot. If you tie a tourniquet above the wound to stanch the flow of blood, eventually the foot will become numb. It will still be wounded, and if you loosen the tourniquet the pain will return, but while the tourniquet remains the pain has vanished. I assume these pellets work in much the same way, but internally rather than externally.''

''It is like magic,'' said Borleshan.

''It is a magic they are willing to share with us,'' answered Lennox.

''I will join you when you speak to Chomanche, and urge him to reach an accommodation with the Men, as long as it is an honorable one. We must have access to this knowledge.''

Shit! It is Chomanche I have to speak to. I wonder exactly what I'll do when I'm close enough to get my hands on him?

''How do you think he will react?'' asked Lennox aloud.

''He has no use for Men,'' replied Borleshan. ''I think it is fair to say that he hates them, especially since the man known as Xavier William Lennox attempted to observe our ceremonies at the pyramid.'' He paused. ''He will not be easy to convince.''

''Perhaps we need a strategy,'' suggested Lennox.

''What kind of strategy?''

"Possibly we should first present our case to others who might view it more favorably, and approach Chomanche with other supporters?"

"Why should Chomanche care?" asked Borleshan curiously. "His word is law."

"What I meant was that where he might not listen to a lone warrior from a distant land and a *raboni* who is obviously beholden to Man's medicine, he might give credence if we present him with ten or twenty *zhandi* whom we have converted to our cause."

"We will make the same arguments to the twenty as to the one," replied Borleshan. "And only the one's answer will matter."

"Do you feel there is a best time to approach him?" queried Lennox.

"What difference will it make? He is Chomanche day and night."

"True," acknowledged Lennox, not willing to push the matter any further.

They reached an oasis an hour later—the water holes came more frequently as they approached what passed for civilization—and although Borleshan wanted to pass it, Lennox insisted that they take a break. He didn't know if he should urge the Firefly to drink, so he simply took a long swallow himself and was gratified to see Borleshan follow suit. The *kadekos* disdained the water, and Lennox decided that thirty minutes' rest was enough.

They trudged on across the desert, which had ceased to be a seemingly endless series of sand dunes and was now simply hard, sun-baked ground, punctuated with tens of thousands of rocks that seemed not to bother the *kadekos* in the least. Lennox constantly scanned the horizon, looking for warriors, *raboni,* anything that could present a problem, but for all he could tell they were the only living things on the face of the planet.

A hot wind began whipping dust into his face, and he found that his eyes possessed a transparent inner membrane that automatically lowered to protect them. Suddenly Lennox was struck by the lunacy of trying to pass himself off as a Firefly when he did not yet know all the functions and facets of his new body. He also considered the question he had not answered the day before: why *was* he here, in this place, in this body, returning to the very spot where he had been maimed? Surely it wasn't for the book; it was already sold. Curiosity? There were other ways to satisfy it. A love of Fireflies? Hardly. He still wasn't sure he wouldn't attack Chomanche the moment he saw him. The simple fact that no one had ever done this before? Hell, no one had ever approached the pyramid before, or done dozens of the things he had done. The more he thought about it, the less he could comprehend his own behavior. He simply knew that the instant Nora Wallace made her offer, he was going to agree, no matter what the hardship.

Or was it the hardship itself that lured him? Angela thought so. For all he knew, so did Nora; she certainly knew what buttons to push. And yet he knew that while he had suffered pain before, and was prepared to do so again, he would much rather *not* undergo any physical discomfort.

Finally disturbed by his inability to come up with an answer, he once again engaged Borleshan in conversation.

"How long do you think it will take us to reach Brakkanan?" he asked.

The Firefly looked at the sky and some distant landmarks that were meaningless to Lennox, whose only previous trip between the outpost and the city had been on foot, in human form.

"We should arrive just before sunset tomorrow," answered Borleshan.

Lennox wanted to ask if he had a place to stay, so that he might suggest remaining with him, but was afraid to display his ignorance. For all he knew the *raboni* slept outside next to their mounts, just as they did in the desert.

"What will you do when we get there?" he asked instead.

"If my comrades are there I will join them."

"And if not?"

Borleshan shrugged. "I will speak to Chomanche with you, and then I will go back into the desert. The city is not for such as me. I do not like the jabbering of females or the mewling of children."

"There are times when I find the companionship of females very pleasant," offered Lennox, trying awkwardly to keep the conversation alive and hoping that the warrior caste hadn't taken some vow of celibacy.

"The companionship, yes; the talk, no. And children are a nuisance; they try my patience."

"Yet without children, there would not be a next generation to do battle."

"I did not say they were not a *necessary* nuisance," replied Borleshan. "Though perhaps they will soon become unnecessary."

"Why should you say that?"

"Because if we can learn Man's art of healing, perhaps no one need ever die, and then what use will we have for children?"

"That would require more than knowledge," said Lennox. "It would take magic."

"Perhaps they possess it," said Borleshan.

"I doubt it."

"You seem to know a lot about them, so if you say they have no magic I will believe you." He stared down at his knee. "But it *seems* like magic."

"Perhaps our pyramid seems like magic to them," suggested Lennox.

"Of course it does," said Borleshan. "Why else would Lennox have approached it? He sensed its power and wished to learn its secrets."

"Perhaps he just wanted to learn about the *zhandi* and what we believe."

"Why?"

"Men collect knowledge. It is their stock in trade."

"Then we must deny it to them."

"Why?"

"Once they know what we know, we have nothing left to trade and they have no reason to let us live."

Close, my friend. Substitute diamonds for knowledge and you've got it.

"Then we shall have to find something that is worthless to us and valuable to them in order to trade," offered Lennox.

"*Is* there such a thing?"

"I'm sure if we search long and hard enough, we will find something."

"I hope so," said the Firefly. "Having experienced the wonders of which they are capable, I would not like to go to war with them."

"I am sure that they, too, prefer peace."

"Perhaps," said Borleshan. "But what you and I and Men want is irrelevant. Chomanche will hear us, and he will decide."

Lennox rode in silence, considering the irony of placing his hopes for peace in the hands of the one Firefly who had already tried to kill him, and would do so again in an instant if he knew what lay beneath the surgically constructed mask that the human wore.

FOURTEEN

The sights and smells of Brakkanan that reached Lennox as he neared the outskirts of the city were much more pleasant than the last time, filtered as they were through his new senses. Colors that once clashed now seemed harmonious. Odors that stung his nostrils now smelled sweet and pure. The sounds of the women working and the children playing were no longer grating. It was strange, but he felt somehow at home.

I'm really going to miss this body. It never tires, and it sees and hears things I never knew existed when I was a Man. It's like I was living in a cocoon until the operation.

He had no idea where he was going, so he slowed his *kadeko* almost imperceptibly and allowed Borleshan to take the lead. The Firefly rode slowly through the main thoroughfares, looking neither right nor left, greeting no one and receiving no greetings in return.

At last they came to a stable and dismounted. Borleshan handed his *kadeko*'s reins to an attendant without saying a word or offering any payment, and Lennox did the same.

"It's time for you to take another pellet," said Lennox.

The Firefly nodded and swallowed a pill.

"I will stay with you," continued Lennox. "You may require help if you plan to do much walking."

"I will see if my clan is here. If they are, they will take care of me."

They walked down another side street to an old, dilapidated building, and entered it. Half a dozen Fireflies were lounging around the totally unfurnished main floor.

"Welcome, Borleshan," said one of them. "We did not expect to see you again."

Lennox assumed that to be the truth, yet if any of them were surprised to see their comrade, they kept it well hidden.

"Dromesche kept his word to me," replied Borleshan, walking around the room for his companions to see. "They repaired my leg."

"It was not Dromesche's word that we doubted, but Man's."

"They promise to cure any injury that any *zhandi* sustains," said Lennox.

"Why should they cure their enemies?" asked another Firefly with an expression of disbelief.

"They are aliens," said Lennox. "You will have to ask *them*."

"What is an alien?" demanded the Firefly sharply. "I have never heard of it."

You put your foot in it again. They don't have a word for alien, *and you used the Terran term without thinking.*

"It is a term Men use for themselves," he said awkwardly.

"You know *too* much about Men," said the Firefly suspiciously.

"I spent much time talking to them while they repaired Borleshan's leg."

"They don't talk to *zhandi*; they kill us."

"That is not so," answered Borleshan. "I was treated with respect while I was among them."

"Because they feared Dromesche," came the answer.

"There were more than one hundred Men there," said Borleshan, "all of them armed. They could have killed us at any time, and yet they chose not to."

"It must be a subterfuge."

"If it is, they have gained nothing by it," said Lennox. "We gave them nothing, and Borleshan can walk again."

"I do not trust them."

"You did not trust me, either, yet I kept my promise to Borleshan," said Lennox.

"I agree with Dromesche," said Borleshan. "Perhaps there is too much mistrust between our races."

"I will trust them only after they leave," said yet another Firefly. "Why are they here in the first place?"

"Ask them," suggested Lennox.

"I do not speak to lesser races."

"Yet this is a lesser race that has knowledge we need," said Borleshan.

"It is also a race that killed seven of us when we caught the intruder, Lennox, approaching the pyramid."

"Believe what you want," said Borleshan. "Dromesche and I will seek out Chomanche to discuss the matter with him, with or without you."

"Without," said a Firefly decisively.

"Chomanche will kill any Man he finds, and he will probably kill both of you for having spoken to them," added another.

Maybe I should cripple Chomanche as I did Borleshan, and then see if he's opposed to talking to human medics. Common sense and self-preservation stopped him from uttering the thought aloud, and he decided to let Borleshan speak for him.

"Then remain here in the shadows, safe and contented and ignorant," said Borleshan. He turned and walked out into the street, and Lennox had no choice but to follow him. He wasn't pleased with this turn of events; no matter what Borleshan thought, he would have felt more comfortable converting a dozen or so *zhandi* to his cause before approaching Chomanche — but if Borleshan couldn't convince his own clan, he didn't see much likelihood of convincing any other Fireflies to join him.

"Let us eat first," said Lennox, who wanted some time to prepare his arguments.

"It is early in the day," noted Borleshan.

"I am nervous about facing Chomanche."

"Pay no heed to my companions. Chomanche will

not kill us for associating with Men.'' Borleshan paused. ''At least, I do not think he will.''

How comforting.

''I am hungry just the same,'' said Lennox. *And I am also curious to see how strangers get a meal in a town that doesn't seem to recognize the concept of restaurants.*

''As you wish,'' said Borleshan.

The Firefly looked into a pair of private domiciles, then chose a third where a female was preparing food.

''Greetings, my sister,'' he said formally. ''May two wayfarers sit at your table?''

''My table is your table,'' said the female, though Lennox could tell from her face and posture that she would have much rather refused. He had a feeling that her religion did not allow her to refuse food or comfort to a fellow Firefly . . . but it could also have been that the *raboni* received special treatment for not stealing within the city limits, or even that Borleshan was personally acquainted with this particular female. He leaned toward the first explanation, but in this silent, mannered society, it was almost impossible for an outsider to comprehend their behavior simply by observing it.

Lennox sat down on a chair that was built for his body—the first he had encountered. It was made of hardwood, and yet it was incredibly comfortable and relaxing. The small seat and high legs accommodated his new pelvis and longer limbs, and his vestigial wings passed through the latticework on the back, rather than being uncomfortably crushed or confined as they were on human furniture. There were no arms to the chair, but his new limbs didn't require them.

Borleshan sat down opposite him, and waited in silence until the female brought them a mushlike concoction in a large bowl. Lennox didn't know what to do with it, so he waited and watched Borleshan. The Firefly pulled the bowl over, stared at its contents, and just when Lennox was sure he was going to lift the huge container to his lips, he stared at the female, who brought two smaller bowls to the table. Borleshan dipped each of them into the container until they were full, then passed one to Lennox and began sipping from the other.

Lennox followed suit, half expecting it to taste like oatmeal, and was surprised to find that it bore a much heartier and more pleasant taste. He thought he was able to differentiate half a dozen subtle spices, and while he couldn't taste any meat, he could almost feel new strength flow through him as his body assimilated the food. Whatever it was, it certainly beat what he had been eating in the desert and at the military outpost.

"Thank you, my sister," said Borleshan, after finishing his meal in total silence.

"Thank you, my sister," repeated Lennox.

"You are welcome, my brothers," she said, inclining her head slightly. "You will be on your way now?"

"Soon," answered Borleshan.

A male Firefly entered the domicile, walked over, and stared at them.

"Greetings, my brothers," he said at last. "I hope you have dined well?"

"Very well," answered Borleshan.

"My domicile is yours," continued the Firefly. "But

of course you have business elsewhere?'' It was a cross between a hint and a hope.

"We have," said Borleshan.

"That is too bad," said the Firefly, looking anything but unhappy. "You must sample our hospitality again."

"Only if we are permitted to return it twofold," said Borleshan.

Evidently that was the expected answer, and, the little ritual done, the Firefly disappeared into another room.

"Well," said Borleshan, looking across the table to Lennox, "I think it is time to be on our way."

"If you say so," replied Lennox.

"You are the leader," said Borleshan. "If you have something more important to tend to . . ."

"No," said Lennox. "Nothing."

They got to their feet. Lennox wondered if he should thank the female, or leave some gift on the table, but Borleshan walked out without a word and Lennox thought it safest to simply follow suit.

They began walking through the twisting streets of Brakkanan. If there was a purpose to the direction the Firefly chose, Lennox couldn't spot it. About the time he was sure that they were thoroughly lost, Borleshan came to a halt in front of a large building.

"He will be in here," announced the Firefly.

Lennox looked at the building. From the exterior it could have been anything: a home, a store, a church, even a stable. It appeared no different in style or design from any of the others, except for its size.

"Then let us speak to him," said Lennox, hoping this was the expected response.

Borleshan entered the building and led Lennox

through a maze of oddly shaped rooms filled with armed Fireflies who stared sullenly at them but made no effort to stop them. Finally they came to a barren room with no windows. A lone Firefly sat against the stone wall, a dull golden blanket wrapped around his shoulders.

Lennox stared at the Firefly. Was this Chomanche? He'd thought the face was burned into his memory, but now that he might actually be confronting him, he couldn't be sure. The Firefly's eyes seemed to bore right through him, but its body seemed even leaner than he remembered. The Firefly didn't show any signs of age—very few of them did—but there was a feeling of weariness about him, as if there was nothing left that could surprise or interest him. The voice, however, was firm and vibrant.

"Why have you intruded upon my solitude?"

"We have matters of great importance to discuss with you, Chomanche," said Borleshan, his body bent in a subservient posture.

"Who are you?"

"I am Borleshan of the Quigada *raboni*."

Chomanche turned to Lennox.

Lennox quickly attempted to imitate Borleshan's posture. "And I am Dromesche, a warrior from a distant land."

"What land?" asked Chomanche.

Lennox tried to remember some of the distant cities his cellmate had mentioned more than a year ago.

"I come originally from Boroda," he responded.

Chomanche nodded. "And you have both come to Brakkanan to seek me out?"

"Yes, Chomanche," said Borleshan.

"Then I will listen to what you have to say."

"We come from the human outpost with a message for you," said Lennox. "A message of peace."

Chomanche merely stared expressionlessly at him.

"This *zhandi*," he continued, indicating Borleshan, "was crippled in a battle less than a month ago. His knee was swollen to three times its normal size. He could not walk, and he was in great agony. I took him to the outpost, and the human doctor cured him." He paused to let the fact sink in. "They have offered to cure any injury suffered by any *zhandi* as a gesture of good faith."

"It is true, Chomanche," continued Borleshan. "At first I doubted Dromesche, but everything he said came to pass. The Men fixed my leg, and treated me with the respect due a *raboni*."

"They feel," added Lennox, "that their motives have been misunderstood. They wish to meet with you and convince you of their good intentions toward the *zhandi*. I have told them that I would convey their message to you."

"They had the opportunity to kill us both, and yet they did not," said Borleshan. "Their medical knowledge is beyond anything we have imagined, and they have offered to trade it to us."

"For what?" asked Chomanche, speaking for the first time.

"I don't know," said Lennox. "But I do know they have no desire to interfere with our society. It is possible they want something that is valuable to them but entirely worthless to us."

"Such as?"

"I don't know," repeated Lennox. "I am not privy to their counsel. I am just a messenger."

"It was you who urged this one"—Chomanche indicated Borleshan—"to trust the humans. Why?"

"I have long observed them," answered Lennox, "and I became convinced that they mean us no harm."

"Despite the number of *zhandi* they have slaughtered?"

"I did not say that they will not fight if they consider themselves provoked," said Lennox. "Merely that their intentions are not hostile. My friend was crippled and in pain. I could not help him. No *zhandi* I knew could help him. There was no one else to ask except the Men."

"*Zhandi* do not ask for help," said Chomanche harshly.

Lennox looked to Borleshan for support, but the Firefly remained silent.

"I asked not for myself," said Lennox, "but for my companion—and the reason I asked was that I was responsible for his injury."

"I am more interested in the Men than in Borleshan's injury," said Chomanche. "They live behind high walls. How were you able to observe them?"

"I have seen them when they were not behind the walls, and have spied upon them. They seemed like reasonable beings."

"They have never seemed so to me," said Chomanche firmly.

"I cannot understand their language, but some actions do not require words. I have seen them resolve their differences through talk, I have seen their doctors treat their sick, I have seen them display compassion not only for each other but even for the beasts of the desert. On two occasions my presence was made known to them, and both times, though they could have killed me, they attempted to communicate with me, and they let me leave unharmed.''

"You say they have no wish to interfere with us," said Chomanche. "And yet they invaded Brakkanan barely half a year ago. What have you to say to that?"

"I was not here, so I do not know all the facts of the matter, but I have been told that they came to rescue a companion.''

"A saboteur.''

"Or perhaps merely a foolish adventurer," offered Lennox. "Did he attempt to harm any *zhandi* or steal anything?"

"We caught him before he had a chance to do so," answered Chomanche.

"Did he admit that this was his purpose?"

"Would you expect a saboteur to admit his purpose?"

"Then it is simply a matter of how you interpret his actions," said Lennox.

Chomanche stared expressionlessly at Lennox for a long moment without speaking. Finally he turned to Borleshan.

"And you—do you agree with Dromesche?"

"Nothing I experienced at the outpost contradicts what he says," answered Borleshan.

"I truly believe they came to Medina with peaceful intentions," said Lennox. "They have opened their hospital to us. Surely we would risk nothing by agreeing to speak to them."

"That is your opinion?" asked Chomanche.

"It is," said Lennox.

"This has been a most illuminating conversation," said Chomanche. He turned to Borleshan. "Borleshan, you will leave us now."

Borleshan immediately left the room.

"He has served his purpose," said Chomanche, staring intently at Lennox. "We no longer need him."

There was a long, uncomfortable silence.

"Have you anything further to ask?" said Lennox, suddenly feeling very uneasy.

"I have just one question," said Chomanche. "Who are you?"

"I told you," said Lennox. "My name is Dromesche."

"I know what you told me. Now I would like you to tell me the truth."

"I don't know what you mean."

"I do not understand how you came to be here in this guise, but you are a Man."

"That's ridiculous!" snapped Lennox with what he hoped was an air of outrage. "Do I look like a Man to you?"

"No," said Chomanche. "But you are a Man nonetheless."

"Why do you insist on saying that?" demanded Lennox.

"When you entered my chamber, I noticed that you awkwardly mimicked Borleshan's gesture of obeisance. That is curious, I thought, for it is taught to all *zhandi* from the time they are small children. I will have to watch this warrior very carefully. But that is only what made me suspicious, not what gave you away.'' The Firefly paused and seemed to look through his skin to the human that lay hidden beneath it. ''The world on which we live is Grotamana,'' he continued. ''Only Men call it Medina.''

Wonderful, Lennox, you goddamned fool! You spent six months preparing for this, and you gave yourself away in less than ten minutes.

FIFTEEN

ᘏᘏᘏᘏᘏᘏᘏᘏᘏᘏᘏᘏ

W ho are you?'' repeated Chomanche, with no change of expression.

''Can't you guess?''

The Firefly considered his answer for a long moment.

''I suspect that you are Xavier William Lennox, but I would like confirmation.''

''I am,'' said Lennox, tensing. ''And remember—I can reach you before any Fireflies can reach *me*.''

''Have you come to kill me?'' asked Chomanche.

''Not unless you force me to,'' said Lennox.

''Are you here for revenge?''

''No.''

Chomanche continued to stare at him. ''This is not a mask or a costume,'' he said at last.

''No.''

''You have actually changed your shape.''

"That's right."

Chomanche reached out and touched him gingerly on the face and torso.

"Lean forward."

Lennox leaned over, and Chomanche examined his wings. Finally he took one of Lennox's lean, long-fingered hands in his own and examined it minutely.

"Magic!" he exclaimed in an awed voice.

"Surgery," replied Lennox.

"What is surgery?"

Lennox began explaining the process, but as he did so the Firefly kept grunting and shaking his head.

"This cannot be true," he interrupted at last. "When I cut off your fingers, you did not grow new ones, either Man's or *zhandi*'s. When I had your foot cut open, a new foot did not appear. No, Dromesche, this is magic."

"It is a scientific procedure."

"What prayers or chants were used?"

"Medical instruments were used, nothing more."

"What instruments?"

"A scalpel—that's a form of knife. And various prosthetics—artificial limbs."

"If I cut you, will you bleed?"

"Yes."

"Then you were deceived," said Chomanche. "Your limbs are not artificial. And if knives were used at all, then doubtless they were blessed by a priest and controlled by God Himself."

I'm never going to win this argument. Besides, why should I bother? If he wants to think God has taken a special interest in me, why disillusion him?

"Only God could create a miracle such as this," continued Chomanche. "It is beyond even the powers of the Pale One."

"The Pale One?" repeated Lennox.

"He who stands opposed to God," answered the priest.

Lennox remained silent as Chomanche reached out and touched him again.

"But *why* has God chosen to make you a *zhandi*?"

All right, we'll play it your way.

"I cannot know what is in the mind of God," said Lennox carefully, hoping he wouldn't be accused of blasphemy, "but I have a theory."

"What is it?"

"I was a Man, and I know that Men are not your enemies," said Lennox. "They wish only to live in peace, and bring you the benefits of their knowledge. But if a Man were to tell you that, you would not believe him. I think God made me a *zhandi* because you would believe the truth only from one of your own people."

Chomanche remained motionless for a long moment, as if coping with the idea.

"It is possible," he said at last.

It is? I wouldn't believe it for two seconds—but then, I'm not a major priest of a backward theocracy.

"It is possible," repeated Chomanche, "but what is possible is not always right. You will live in my home, dine at my table, and before we are through I will know exactly why God has sent you here in this form."

"I accept your hospitality," said Lennox. *As if I had any choice in the matter.* "I have much to learn from you, for while I am physically a *zhandi,* mentally I am still a Man, and there is much that I don't understand.''

''From this moment forward, you are no longer Xavier William Lennox the Man, but rather Dromesche the *zhandi,*'' announced Chomanche. ''And since God has transformed you and sent you to me, I will guide you along the path to true knowledge until I can divine His purpose.''

''Let's start now,'' said Lennox, pushing his advantage. ''Why did you mutilate me?''

''Obviously God was testing us.''

''But you didn't know that at the time,'' persisted Lennox. ''I meant you no harm. If God did not tell you to do it . . .''

''It was done for reasons of political expediency, of course,'' concluded Chomanche. ''It is the same reason you were allowed to live.''

''Allowed?'' said Lennox. ''You were just about to kill me when my rescuers arrived!''

''We saw them coming when they were halfway between Brakkanan and the pyramid,'' said Chomanche. ''Do you really think a body of warriors can sneak up on a *zhandi* at night?''

Of course—my night vision! Why the hell didn't I think of that?

''Or that I could not have killed you with a single spear thrust before they arrived?''

More than half a year of dwelling upon it, and it never once occurred to me.

''I'd still like an explanation.''

''Supply it yourself, Dromesche,'' said the Firefly.

"One thing I know: God would not turn a fool into a *zhandi*."

Don't bet on it.

"Killing me would precipitate a war?"

"Do you really think Xavier William Lennox was that important?"

"No," answered Lennox honestly. "Probably not."

Chomanche said nothing.

"I was a warning," said Lennox after a moment's consideration.

"Of course."

Lennox frowned in confusion. "But the garrison knew you didn't want intruders, and you knew I wasn't a member of the military, so that doesn't make any sense."

The Firefly sat motionless, as if waiting for Lennox to speak again.

"It wasn't the *garrison* you were warning," Lennox said slowly, working through his thoughts. "You knew who I was, and you knew my reputation. You knew I would take my story back to my people. You wanted me to tell it so that no other Men would come to Medina."

Chomanche grunted an affirmative.

"So even if the outpost hadn't sent soldiers to rescue me, you were never going to kill me."

"What would be the point?"

"Whereas if I had been a soldier, you'd have killed me on the spot?"

"That would have meant a change in Man's policy, and we would have gone to war."

"But since I was famous, and not in the military, I was worth more to you alive and disfigured than dead."

Chomanche saw no need to confirm the obvious, and remained silent.

"It makes sense," admitted Lennox.

"You have no anger?"

"Anger is like pain," said Lennox. "Eventually it passes."

"Good," said Chomanche. "It would not be beyond our God to have sent you here to punish us." He paused. "What is it that you want from me?"

"I want to learn from you," said Lennox. "I am half a *zhandi*; I wish to become a whole one. I already see and hear and feel things as a *zhandi;* now I want to interpret them as a *zhandi*. I want to know what you know, think as you think."

And if I find it as fulfilling as wearing one of your bodies, I may never go back.

"I will instruct you," said Chomanche. "And, in return, you will teach me what you know of Men, so that I will not be at a disadvantage should I choose to meet with them."

Suddenly the priest stood up and clapped his hands. A moment later some two dozen *zhandi* filed into the room. Lennox assumed that the armed ones were warriors and the rest were priests.

"This is Dromesche," announced Chomanche. "Mark him well and remember him, for he has been chosen by God to walk among us. If he asks for help, you must give it to him. If he seeks knowledge, you will not withhold it. If he transgresses our laws, you will report such transgressions to me, but will take no action against him."

An old priest, his body stooped in a posture of extreme subservience, spoke in barely audible tones. "I would never doubt the word of Chomanche," he whispered cautiously, "but Dromesche looks like any other *zhandi*. May I ask in what way he has been chosen by God?"

"Look at Dromesche carefully," said Chomanche. "Do any of you recognize him?"

The assembled priests and warriors all muttered negative answers.

"You are wrong," said Chomanche.

"I have never seen him before," said a warrior.

"Yes, you have," replied Chomanche. "You even thrust a spear through his foot."

"If he told you that, he is lying!" protested the warrior.

"No, he is not," said Chomanche. "There is a witness."

"Who?" demanded the warrior.

"Myself."

The warrior could not bring himself to contradict the high priest, but his demeanor showed total confusion and disbelief.

"You asked how I know he was chosen," continued Chomanche, turning back to the old priest. "Now you shall have your answer. Dromesche, tell them your former name."

"Xavier William Lennox," said Lennox.

Lennox looked at the faces of the assembled *zhandi*.

I'll be damned! Not a single one of them is going to challenge it. Not only that—I think they actually believe him! One word from the high priest and it's law. No wonder they're still riding kadekos *and shitting out-doors.*

"Why has he been sent here?" asked a priest.

"That is for me to interpret in the fullness of time," said Chomanche before Lennox had a chance to answer. "But remember his face and remember my instructions."

Chomanche made a dismissive gesture, and the room immediately emptied out.

"I have some more questions," said Lennox.

"God could have given you the answers to your questions, just as He gave you a new body," replied Chomanche. "The fact that He did not means that He wants you to learn the answers for yourself."

"That's what I'm trying to do."

Chomanche got to his feet. "The first thing I must teach you is patience. You spent your entire life as a Man; you cannot spiritually become a *zhandi* in a matter of days or months." He paused. "I could answer every question you have about the *zhandi* before nightfall, and my answers would be useless to you. You must spend time living among us, not merely observing but *experiencing.*"

"I plan to."

"Come," said Chomanche, walking to the doorway. "It is time to show you to your quarters."

Lennox arose and followed the priest through the crowded rooms leading to the street.

"I had thought *this* was your home," said Lennox.

"You were wrong."

"Is it a place of worship?"

"Perhaps tomorrow you shall tell *me* what it is."

They walked in silence, following the winding street, then turning onto a side street. They stopped at a building that seemed no grander than any other.

"We are here," announced Chomanche. "Come, Dromesche."

The Firefly entered the building, and Lennox fell into step behind him. They passed through an unfurnished room, then a sweet-smelling kitchen in which two females were working; both ignored him. Then they came to a row of three rooms with mats on the floor. Chomanche led him through all three, to a small, circular chamber with two small windows.

"You will sleep here," said Chomanche.

Lennox looked around silently.

"Do I sense that you are displeased?"

"One room's as good as another," replied Lennox. "But if I should wish to leave during the night, I must pass through all the other rooms. I don't wish to disturb your sleep."

"Why would you leave?"

"Learning is not a process that stops at sunset."

"Each night you will go to the pyramid," said Chomanche. "And since I will be there too, you will not awaken me."

"I will be allowed to go?" asked Lennox, surprised.

"You are a *zhandi*," answered the priest, dismissing the question.

"I will not know what to do when I get there."

"What did you plan to do the last time you were there?"

"Join the crowd and imitate them until I understood what was happening."

"A reasonable procedure."

"That's all you're going to tell me?" asked Lennox.

"If you make an earnest effort and still have difficulty, then I will guide you," answered Chomanche.

"I have a feeling that no matter how much I assimilate on my own, there is one thing you will eventually have to explain to me," said Lennox.

"What is that?"

"Why those two *zhandi* willingly jumped to their deaths."

"Perhaps I will have to tell you," agreed Chomanche. "But if you can comprehend it without my help, on that day you will truly be a *zhandi* in spirit as well as body."

Lennox made a silent promise to himself that there would come a day when he would stand atop the pyramid and know the answer to his question.

SIXTEEN

Lennox stood atop the massive pyramid and looked out across the desert with his artificial eyes. He surveyed the midday sky, the clouds, the shifting sands, the town of Brakkanan some three miles distant. Then he closed his eyes and fluttered his vestigial wings.

Nothing happened.

What did they see? Did they think they could fly? Did they realize they were leaping to their deaths? And if they didn't realize it here, how about when they were halfway down? Did they regret it then—or was death what they wanted?

He opened his eyes and looked down at the ground. There was no sense of vertigo, no fear that he might lose his balance.

What makes a man, or a zhandi, *willingly jump from this height? Had they reached such a moment of insight or exultation that they knew nothing they ever experienced in the future could equal it? Did they see that the theocracy had made their lives meaningless, and jump because there was no way to change their fate?*

He'd been going to the pyramid every night for a week. The prayers still made no sense to him, but he understood the form of the ceremony and had no difficulty becoming one of the thousands who participated in the nightly ritual. Yet not a single night had gone by without two or three *zhandi* climbing to the very top of the pyramid, standing exactly where he was standing now, and hurling themselves off into space. They were not sacrifices. No one forced them to do what they did. Nor were they drugged. They were clear-headed adults; they did not seem especially overcome with religious fervor; they had no more reason to die than they had had a day or a week or a month earlier. And yet they had jumped.

Lennox looked down and saw a solitary figure approaching the pyramid, leading a *kadeko*. His human vision could never have identified it, but his new eyes saw clearly that it was Borleshan, with whom he had lost contact since his first day in Brakkanan. He yelled a greeting, waved as the Firefly looked up, and began climbing down the steps at the back of the pyramid.

"They told me I would find you here," said Borleshan, as Lennox finally reached the ground and approached him. "I have come to say good-bye."

"You are going back to the desert with your *raboni*?"

"There is nothing in the city to hold us here. I find it . . . confining."

"How is your knee?"

"The pain is all but gone."

"I am glad to hear that," said Lennox. "I hope you fare well."

"I would wish you the same," answered Borleshan, "but the Chosen of God does not need the wishes of a *raboni*."

"The Chosen of God?"

"That is how they refer to you, Xavier William Lennox, and that is another reason I must leave."

"I don't understand," said Lennox.

"Chomanche has convinced the priests that you have been transformed into a *zhandi* by God. Since I have traveled with you, I am constantly being asked to recount our adventures."

And you couldn't lie to save your soul.

"I see," said Lennox.

"I don't think you do," responded Borleshan. "I have seen the wonders of Man's medicine at first hand, and I believe I know how your metamorphosis was accomplished. Yet to suggest it, to say something, *any*thing, contradictory to what Chomanche has proclaimed, would be to forfeit my life as a blasphemer. Far better to be out in the desert, among my own kind, where hopefully the subject will never arise."

Lennox extended his hand.

"What does this mean?" asked the Firefly.

"It's a human gesture. Take it."

Borleshan took his hand.

"It means that we are friends, and that I wish you well," said Lennox.

"I do not know exactly why you are here, Xavier William Lennox, but Men have treated me fairly. I hope you succeed in your mission, whatever it is. I will watch from afar, but with interest.''

Borleshan turned and walked off toward his *kadeko*, and rather than climb the pyramid again, Lennox began the dusty trek back to Brakkanan.

I love these inner eyelids, he thought as the wind whipped past him. *I wonder why we couldn't engineer them for all humans who work on desert worlds? And the legs—I must weigh more now than I did as a Man, but they never seem to tire.* He felt an urge to jog to the city, just to test his endurance, but thought better of it. This was a strictly regulated society, and any breach of those regulations was likely to be taken as an act of blasphemy. One didn't jog, or wrap one's robe differently, or suggest civic improvements—and only Lennox, by grace of God and Chomanche, seemed to be able to ask questions with impunity.

When he was halfway to Brakkanan, he changed directions and decided to walk in a huge circle around the city.

It's strange, but I, too, find Brakkanan confining, though I suspect for different reasons than Borleshan does. I love the feeling of freedom and power this body gives me, but there is so little freedom in this society that I feel constricted, physically as well as mentally. There are so many things a Firefly can do with this body, and yet so few that he is permitted to do. . . .

He reached Chomanche's home shortly before dark, and joined the priest at the dinner table. The two females served their food, as they had every night.

''I have a question,'' said Lennox when the females had vanished back into the recesses of the kitchen.

"You may ask."

"Are they your wives?"

"Yes."

"Why do they not dine with us?"

"They are females."

"Do not females get hungry too?" asked Lennox, hoping to hide the sardonicism from his voice.

"They are neither our physical nor mental equals," answered Chomanche. "It is best that they live apart from us."

"Do you school them as you do your young males?"

"Certainly not. The effort would be wasted."

"And may I assume that they are not given positions of responsibility in your society?"

"They would prove inadequate," said Chomanche firmly.

"I see."

"You disapprove?"

"It is not for me to say," replied Lennox. "I am simply trying to learn."

"We are alone. You may speak frankly."

Lennox picked up a small water gourd. "If you were denied an education, and refused any possibility of a responsible position in Brakkanan, why would you grow up to be any more intelligent or useful than this gourd?"

"Our females *are* educated," responded Chomanche patiently. "They are taught how to cook and sew from earliest childhood, and before they reach childbearing age they know how to care for infants."

I'll bet they're really good at hauling firewood, too.

"Obviously I misunderstood you," said Lennox.

''Men train their females the same way they train their males?'' asked Chomanche.

''Yes, they do.''

The priest considered it for a moment, then shrugged. ''They are a different race.''

Well, at least it's not blasphemous. There may be hope for you yet.

''Tell me more about Men,'' said Chomanche, after a thoughtful silence.

''What do you wish to know?''

''They have spread throughout the galaxy, have they not?''

''Yes.''

''How many worlds are in their Republic?''

''The last I heard, there were about twelve thousand,'' answered Lennox. ''The figure may have risen by a few hundred in the past year.''

''Since they hunger for so many worlds, why should I believe that they do not hunger for mine?''

''Men assimilate no world into the Republic that does not wish to be assimilated,'' said Lennox. ''The world must vote to become a member of the Republic, and that vote must be ratified by Man's government on Deluros VIII.''

''We do not wish to be assimilated,'' said Chomanche. ''I have told them so. If you are speaking the truth, why do they not leave?''

''It must be that you have something they wish to trade for,'' answered Lennox. ''If that is so, you are in a particularly enviable position.''

''Explain.''

''While you can trade only those things that exist

upon Grotamana, they can trade goods from more than twelve thousand worlds.'' Lennox paused, trying to determine if he was making any progress, but Chomanche's face was an impassive mask. ''They can also trade something that is unique in the galaxy: their knowledge.''

''We have no interest in their knowledge,'' said Chomanche.

''I think you might wish to reconsider,'' continued Lennox. ''They have already made their medical facilities available to all *zhandi*. They can teach your people what they know about the science of healing. It would spell an end to much death and suffering.''

''I have already ordered my people not to visit your outpost,'' said Chomanche.

''Why?''

''Because your medicine is contrary to God's will. If He ordains that we must suffer and die, who are we to circumvent His desires?''

''Perhaps He desires you to learn how to make sick *zhandi* well, or He would not have allowed Men to make such an offer to you.''

Chomanche shook his head. ''That is the work of the Pale One, who always offers us the easy path. God's desires are manifest: when you are visited with illness or injury, it is because you have transgressed His laws, and must suffer the consequences of your actions.''

And putting that knowledge in the hands of someone else would dilute the power of the priesthood, wouldn't it?

''Then, as I say, consider the fact that you will have the goods from thousands of worlds to choose from.''

"God created us and Grotamana," said Chomanche. "What else could we need?"

So says the priest who has never even left this city, let alone the planet.

"There are so many things," replied Lennox. "Fabrics that the wind cannot tear. Dyes that the weather cannot dim. Machines that can go where *kadekos* cannot go, and never tire."

"And weapons?"

"Weapons, too."

"What *kind* of weapons?"

It's always weapons, isn't it?

Lennox described some of the simpler firearms in detail. The priest seemed impressed.

"And what will Men ask of us in exchange?"

"I do not know," said Lennox.

"Guess, then."

"There are many minerals . . ." he began.

"Minerals?" interrupted Chomanche.

"Stones of different textures. There are many of them that Men find desirable."

"For personal decoration?"

"Among other things."

"We have very few such stones."

"Men have machines that can detect them even when they are buried in the ground, or hidden inside the walls of caves. It is possible that they will offer you many things that are of very little interest or worth to them, or things that they possess in great quantity, in exchange for these stones that are of no worth to you."

Chomanche merely stared at him expressionlessly, and Lennox felt compelled to continue, to list as many things as possible that Men might want so the priest wouldn't place too high a value on the diamonds they were really after. When he had exhausted all the possibilities—there weren't all that many on this barren, arid world—the priest remained silent for a few moments, then stood up.

"I will think about it."

Sure you will, you sly old bastard. And then you'll find some reason to reverse your position and trade for guns.

Lennox went to bed, wondering if he had handled the situation correctly. He found out the next morning, when Chomanche sought him out.

"I have thought about it, and I will speak to the Men," announced the priest.

Too easy. You've got some escape clause hidden up your nonexistent sleeve.

"I am very glad to hear it," said Lennox.

"You will arrange a meeting with them here in Brakkanan. Since they are the intruders, we will permit only two of them to come, and they must be unarmed. You will go to their fortress and bring them, and you will act as their interpreter."

"I will be happy to."

"If more than two come, or they have hidden weapons, or they demand concessions rather than trade, I will know that you have forsaken God for the Pale One, and the pain you suffered as Xavier William Lennox will be as nothing compared to that which you shall suffer as Dromesche."

So much for being Chosen of God.

"I understand," said Lennox. "When do you want to meet with them?"

"You have been among us for seven days. I do not wish them to think I am too eager, so you will wait for twenty more days before leaving for their fortress."

"As you wish," said Lennox. "Is there anything more?"

"Just this," said Chomanche. "God has given you the body of a *zhandi,* and I have treated you as such."

"I appreciate it."

The priest raised his hand. "I am not through." He stared intently into Lennox's artificial eyes. "Men are a vicious, duplicitous race, and you are still half a Man. I shall be observing you *very* closely."

SEVENTEEN

The Men came and the Men left, and they came again, and finally a deal was struck. The Republic obtained the right to mine diamonds in the desert beyond Brakkanan, and Chomanche received one hundred firearms per year—which he promptly put in the hands of the truest of the true believers.

As for Lennox, he had accomplished his mission in less than two months. He was free to return home and have the surgery reversed, but he was reluctant to give up his new body, and he still had much to learn about the Fireflies of Medina.

One of the things he had always wondered about was the fact that his body, like all the others, glowed in the dark. Eventually he pieced together the reason: in antiquity there had been a nocturnal predator, long since extinct, that hunted the Fireflies. Somewhere along the evolutionary path they had developed the ability to glow, which virtually blinded the huge-eyed predator.

(A valuable by-product of the ability to glow was that it made theft, and most other lawbreaking, virtually impossible, since there was no way to operate in secret by day or by night. Thus, there was no law enforcement body and no court system, since almost all crimes involved some form of blasphemy and were handled by the priesthood.)

The wings were another matter. They were never intended for flight, and no one could offer a reasonable suggestion for their existence. Lennox could flutter his wings with a conscious effort, but it served no purpose: they didn't cool him, they were not capable of protecting his bare skin from insects on those occasions when he removed his robes, and they gave him no illusion that he might be capable of flight.

At the same time that he was exploring the limits of his remarkable body, testing its strength, its vision, its ability to digest almost anything, he was also exploring the much more confining limits of the society in which he found himself.

Literacy was limited to the priests, and they read only one thing—their holy book, which was the only book one could find in Brakkanan.

Everything that was not easily explained, be it natural phenomena or Man's technology, was credited to magic.

Children ran wild in the streets, walking into any house they chose for meals, frequently remaining in strangers' houses for the night. Parents didn't seem to worry about their absence, nor did they feel any sense of possession or responsibility. Any adult of either sex could give a child a blow on the side of the head for not obeying an order fast enough, and the children seemed to accept it with neither surprise nor resentment.

Females avoided him, and felt uncomfortable in his presence. They would answer his questions—after all, Chomanche had ordered all his people to do so—but Lennox could tell that their only close contact with males of the species was for procreation. By the time a female had reached childbearing age, she knew her place in the society and would never dream of challenging the existing order of things. Once, when Lennox saw a female staggering under an enormous burden, he offered to help her carry it, and was threatened by a passing male who backed off only when he recognized the Chosen of God. (That same night Chomanche explained to him that females were sturdy creatures who required no help in their daily chores, and could only be spoiled and/or corrupted by behavior such as he had exhibited earlier in the day.)

All commerce was carried on by barter, but unlike the exotic marketplaces on Binder X and Kennedy II and Greenveldt, there was such a paltry selection of items to trade—and such an abundance of those items in the marketplace—that a simple transaction frequently took all day, and involved each participant's visiting dozens of traders to get a minimally better deal. When Lennox suggested that all of the merchants dealing in a certain desert fruit pool their merchandise and set a firm price, they looked at him as if he was crazy, listened politely because he was Blessed, and went back to doing business as usual as soon as he walked away.

The more time he spent among the Fireflies, the happier he was that the outpost had weapons to trade for the diamonds, for as far as he could tell, the Fireflies neither wanted nor needed anything else. There was too much land and too few inhabitants for there to be any wars. There was enough water—barely—to go around. *Kadekos* reproduced quickly, and were easy to come by. The ramshackle dwellings protected the Fireflies from the sun and the wind. The few irrigated orchards and the various meat animals provided more than enough to eat. That was the basic starting point for most civilizations, but it seemed to be the apex of this one.

The only thing that seemed to matter to them was their religion, and it remained a mystery to him. He had laboriously translated the first quarter of the holy book, and found an unexceptional creation myth and a number of moral parables, most of them involving the painful death of anyone who questioned the teachings of the major prophets and lawgivers.

The book told the Fireflies what to eat, how to dress, when to procreate, what to think—and, perhaps even more important, what *not* to think. The more he learned, the more he regretted having this body in this society, for under other circumstances he might well have considered staying, if not for the rest of his life, at least for a few years, but the oppressive stagnation brought about by the religion made him feel intellectually claustrophobic.

He decided that he would remain just long enough to comprehend the initial mystery that had brought him back: the reason that two or three or more Fireflies plunged to their deaths from atop the pyramid every night.

He asked the priests about it, but they would only answer that there would come a time when he would understand, and would perhaps even feel the need to take that final jump himself.

Speaking to the ordinary Fireflies didn't add much to his knowledge. They understood that any of them might feel the urge to leap off the pyramid any given evening, but they couldn't tell him why—and since no one ever survived the plunge, he couldn't question anyone who had done it.

Each morning found him climbing the stairs to the top, staring out across the desert, and wondering what it was that the Fireflies saw or felt.

Then one morning, as he was standing there, he became aware of another presence, and turned to find a familiar-looking Firefly standing a few feet away, staring at him.

"Greetings, Xavier William Lennox," said the Firefly.

"Greetings," replied Lennox, staring at him.

"Do you not recognize me?"

"I know I have seen you before," said Lennox. "But I cannot recall where."

"I am Jamarsh, one of the traders you befriended in the desert."

"Of course," said Lennox. "Please forgive me."

"There is nothing to forgive," said Jamarsh. "You are the Chosen of God."

"How are your companions, Neshbidan and Sumriche?"

"They are well. We have been to Kannagen and Plistanan and Corbedian, and have just now returned to Brakkanan, to find that Chomanche now speaks with Men and brandishes their weapons."

"Why did they not come here with you?"

"They are afraid to be seen by you."

"Afraid of me?" said Lennox, surprised. "Why? I carry no weapons."

"They are ashamed that they did not recognize you as the Chosen of God."

"I am glad that you are not afraid of me."

"I see no reason to be. God gave me no sign that you were Xavier William Lennox rather than Dromesche. Therefore, to see through His ruse might well have been blasphemous."

This God of yours is a mighty handy guy to have around, thought Lennox wryly. *He not only excuses ignorance—He demands it.*

Aloud he said: "Why have you come to the pyramid, Jamarsh?"

"To see you," said the Firefly.

"Here I am."

"They told me you come here every day."

"That's true."

"May I ask why?"

"Curiosity. I want to learn all there is to know about being a *zhandi,* and I feel I can't do that until I know why your people willingly leap to their deaths from here."

"You will never know," said Jamarsh.

"Even though I am Chosen by God?"

"There is a difference between being Chosen by God,

and being God himself. God is complete. You are not.''

''I think you are mistaken. Not about my not being God, of course, but about my being incomplete. If I was missing something, you would have spotted it the first day we met.''

''I cannot see what you are missing,'' said Jamarsh. ''But then, neither can you.''

''I don't understand you.''

''You are destined never to know why the *zhandi* leap to their deaths, because to do so you must be a *zhandi* yourself. And how can you, who lived your life as a Man, truly be a *zhandi* when your presence among us turned Chomanche into half a Man?''

That was when Lennox knew that it was time to go home.

EIGHTEEN

Angela Stone stood staring at the hideous creature seated on the couch.

"Well?" she demanded. "I'm waiting for an answer."

The creature stared at her expressionlessly and made no reply.

"Damn it, Xavier! You've been back two months and I haven't seen a single page."

"That's not a question," said Lennox placidly.

"Have you even started writing the book yet?"

"No."

"When *do* you plan to start? Your publisher is getting anxious, and frankly, so am I."

"I don't plan to."

"*What?*"

"You heard me. I'm not writing the book."

"Why the hell not?"

"I don't know enough yet," replied Lennox. "Probably I never will."

"What kind of answer is that?" snapped Angela.

"An honest one."

"Look," she said, "it's bad enough that you still look like something out of everyone's worst nightmare. You sit around the house, you don't speak or correspond with anyone, you don't answer your calls or your mail." She paused. "I hope to hell you're going to go back to being the old Xavier after the operation."

"The old Xavier only dabbled on the surface of things," said Lennox.

"The old Xavier wrote four best-selling books and had an appreciative audience of more than a million readers."

"I read them again last week."

"And?"

"I burned them."

"You burned them?" she repeated.

"They were trivial."

"Did they operate on your brain, too?" said Angela in frustration.

"Not at all. They gave me some new senses, and Medina gave me a lot to think about."

"You can't give a brain new senses."

"Then they gave me a new way of using old ones," said Lennox. "Turn off the lights."

"I know—you can see in the dark."

"So can you, if you're near me." He tried to contort his face into some semblance of a smile. "I glow now."

"So now you can do some parlor tricks. Wonderful. What about your book? What about *you*?"

"What about me?"

"You're just not the same man who left for that damned surgery a year ago. I don't know if they've added something, or taken something away, but you're *different*."

"Of course I'm different!" He stood up and faced her. "Look at me."

"You're different on the *inside*."

"Perhaps." Lennox was silent for a moment. "Have you ever walked across a desert?"

"Of course not."

"I did. It was fifty-eight degrees Celsius, and the waterholes were thirty miles apart."

"It sounds horrible!"

"It does, doesn't it?" replied Lennox. "I found it exhilarating."

"I suppose you had sex with some lady Fireflies, too."

Lennox shook his head. "It's a strict, puritanical society. It simply isn't done." He paused. "But during my last week or two there, the idea seemed less repugnant to me."

"I'm sure it did," she said caustically.

"Well, it's only natural. I've been a year without sex."

"Don't go looking at *me*."

He stared at her for a long, uncomfortable moment. "You look . . . *fit*."

Now it was her turn to stare at him. "Just fit? Nothing more?"

He shrugged. "Healthy."

"You've got a serious problem, Xavier."

"You can help me solve it after the operation. For old time's sake."

"I think not."

"As you wish. I was just being polite; I didn't really mean it."

"I know."

"Do you know what I mind the most?" he said. "I've got these fantastic reflexes, this phenomenal eyesight and night vision and hearing, this remarkable endurance—and I've no *use* for them here."

"You're on a civilized world," answered Angela. "You don't need them. We stopped evolving when we invented the wheel and climate control."

"But it's such a *waste*! What's the use of having them if I can't put them to use?"

"None. That's why you're going to reverse the operation and become a man again. I think you'd better get psychological counseling, too."

Lennox sat back down on his chair, crushing his wings against his back. He stared at his alien hands for a moment, then looked up. "Yeah, I know."

"But?"

"I beg your pardon?"

"It sounded like you wanted to add a 'but.' "

"But I'm going to miss having these abilities," replied Lennox.

"You don't need them," said Angela.

"I know."

"Then why are you so depressed?"

"Are you planning on having any children in the future?" asked Lennox.

"No."

"How would you like to have your breasts surgically removed?"

"That's not the same thing, Xavier."

"No, it isn't. You've *never* used them."

"This is a silly conversation," said Angela.

"I didn't start it."

"Look, if it means that much to you, why not tell them to let you keep your night vision and some of the other things?"

Lennox sighed. "To what purpose? If I want to see at night, I can turn a light on."

"Then what *do* you want?"

"I don't know."

But he did.

NINETEEN

Lennox ignored the awed and occasionally terrified stares as he was ushered down the hospital corridor and into the small, makeshift office. A short, chunky woman rose from behind her desk and walked forward to greet him as the door shut behind him.

"Good afternoon, Mister Lennox," said Nora Wallace. "I am so glad to see you again."

"Why did you want to see me at all?" he asked. "Your department debriefed me for damned near four days when I got back."

"I know. I would like to add my congratulations to theirs. What you did was extraordinary. We obtained the diamond concession without having to involve the military—and you accomplished it in less than two months! Most remarkable!" She gestured to a chair that had been constructed especially to accommodate his Firefly body. "Won't you please sit down?"

Lennox took a seat, and waited for her to do the same.

"Are you thirsty?" she asked solicitously.

"In *this* body?" he asked with a dry laugh.

"I'm sorry it has taken so long to schedule your surgery," continued Nora, "but Doctor Ngoni was on vacation, and I didn't trust anyone else to do the job. I'm sure you must be very anxious to become a Man again."

"Very," he replied tonelessly.

"Of course, you *could* have contacted us last month, rather than waiting for us to get in touch with you."

Lennox stared at his long, inhuman fingers. "I was busy."

"And how is your book coming along?"

He shrugged noncommittally.

"I would love to see some pages if they're available."

"I'm still researching it."

"You're researching your own firsthand experiences as a Firefly?" she asked with a disbelieving expression.

"I don't tell you how to do your job," said Lennox irritably. "Don't tell me how to do mine."

"I certainly meant no offense, Mister Lennox," said Nora. There was a long, uncomfortable pause. "Have you any questions about the surgery?"

"None."

"I thought you would be more excited about returning to human form."

"I suppose it has its advantages," said Lennox.

"And its disadvantages?"

"Those too."

"Perhaps you might like to enumerate them for me."

"Why bother?"

"I have my reasons."

Lennox shrugged. "I have a feeling that I'll never fit in again as a Man—not that I fit in all that well before the surgery."

"Why do you think that?" asked Nora.

"I've experienced too many things that no other Man will ever experience," he replied. "I've seen things they'll never see, done things they'll never do—that they *can't* do with Men's bodies. I've lived as an alien. I've stood atop a pyramid from which Fireflies willingly leap to their deaths every day. I've broken bread—or the equivalent—with a tribe of alien outlaws and with a priest of a religion no Man will ever comprehend, and been accepted as a Firefly by both. How can I fit in after all that?"

"But surely you can adjust," she said. "I mean, isn't it like coming back from a vacation—or, in your case, an adventure—that most people will never experience?"

He shook his head. "No. When you've taken a vacation or undergone an adventure, there's always a chance that someone else might share those experiences in the future. Or that you will meet someone who has been to the same places or done the same or similar things. But no Man will ever become a Firefly. They'll never know what it is to walk and breathe and eat in a Firefly's body."

"What was *your* reaction to it?" asked Nora. "Did you enjoy it?"

He paused thoughtfully. "I don't think *enjoy* is the

right word. I learned, on my last day there, that I would be forever as incomplete as a Firefly as I will be as a Man. I didn't belong there, any more than I belong here.'' He shrugged once more. ''I suppose some people are destined not to belong, wherever they are.''

''What do you plan to do now?''

''I don't know.''

''Explore more worlds?''

''No, I don't think so.''

''Do alien worlds no longer hold any appeal for you?''

''Yes.'' Then, ''No.'' Then, ''Now that I've experienced one as a native, I realize how inadequate it is to try to learn about them as a Man.''

She stared at him for a long moment. ''Would you prefer to remain in *this* body?''

''No,'' he said. ''I'll miss some of its abilities, but this body belongs on Medina. It has even less business being on a human world than *I* do.''

Nora Wallace was silent, and suddenly Lennox became aware of the fact that she was leaning back in her chair and smiling at him.

''What's so funny?'' he demanded.

''I'm just amazed at how close your reactions are to your psychological profile.''

''I don't think I follow you.''

''Do you remember that battery of tests you took before your surgery?'' asked Nora. ''They not only told us that you would adapt to being a Firefly, but they also predicted your behavior upon returning from your assignment.''

"I've been here for five minutes," said Lennox. "What do *you* know of my behavior?"

"I know that you haven't written a word. I know that you are unhappy at the thought of remaining a Firefly and equally unhappy about once again becoming a Man. I know that *we* had to contact *you* about this evening's surgery, that you made no attempt to hasten the process. I know that—"

"All right," he interrupted her angrily. "So your shrinks are good at their work. So what?"

"So I have a proposition for you, Mister Lennox."

Suddenly Lennox tensed. "Yes?"

"Your choice of bodies needn't be limited to Man and Firefly."

"Go on," said Lennox, hoping his alien voice wasn't betraying his excitement.

"The Department of Alien Affairs is very pleased with the job you did," she said. "If you're interested, we would consider collaborating with you on another such mission."

"Where?"

"We have a choice of four worlds at present," she replied. "In each case, you would represent the Republic's interests." She paused. "Doctor Ngoni and her staff are prepared to turn you into an inhabitant of whichever world you choose. Or, if you aren't interested, we will honor our word and turn you back into Xavier William Lennox."

"Which four worlds?" he asked, ignoring her final statement.

Nora activated her computer. "I can show you on this."

"I want to keep my night vision," said Lennox suddenly. "And my reflexes. And I still want to see into the infrared." He paused thoughtfully. "And I want more fingers. Or tentacles. Or whatever they use to manipulate things."

"We're limited to the races that we're dealing with," she replied. "Perhaps you'd like to see some holographs of them?"

"Yes."

"And recordings of their major languages. We certainly don't want to send you someplace where you can't understand what they're saying."

"I'll understand," he said with certainty.

"Once you've made your selection, you'll have to undergo another interview with Doctor Ngoni, who will explain what the surgical procedure entails, and of course you'll have to sign another release."

"Yes, yes, yes," said Lennox distractedly. "Now show me the races."

"I'll be happy to," said Nora. "First, I just want to tell you how much I will enjoy working with you again."

"Who'd have thought I'd be doing this again?" mused Lennox in happy wonderment.

"Who indeed?" replied Nora with a smile as the computer displayed a holograph of a delicate, multicolored, inhuman form.

TWENTY

❧❧❧❧❧❧❧❧❧❧❧❧

He bore absolutely no resemblance to a Firefly—but then, Artismo bore absolutely no resemblance to Medina. It was a wet, steaming, jungle world, filled with strange creatures. And Lennox was in the body of the strangest of all, a sentient race that the Pioneer Corps had dubbed Hawkhorns.

In fact, he was there to secure the release of four members of the Pioneer team that had been mapping the planet when they were attacked and taken prisoner by the Hawkhorns. No ransom had been demanded, and since the Hawkhorns refused to speak to human diplomats, it had been decided to send in a surrogate Hawkhorn—Lennox—to assess the situation and bring the prisoners out.

At least this body was designed to let Lennox do the job. It was short and squat, and tremendously powerful, capable of lifting enormous weights and delivering killing blows to creatures much larger than itself. The skin was thick and plated, almost like armor, and—except for his face, the palms of his hands, and the soles of his feet—it was covered with short feathers that formed a riotous pattern of yellows, oranges, and blues and protected him from the constant rain.

He decided early on that he liked his feet. As he walked through the rain forest, his great weight would force his feet six and eight inches into the mud. As they went down they splayed slightly, and when he lifted them they immediately returned to their original shape, so that he never found himself stuck and unable to move.

He had two opposing thumbs on each hand, and it wasn't long before he wondered how Man had ever accomplished so much with only one thumb per hand. Despite his huge size and heavy bone structure, his hands were capable of the most delicate manipulations.

The bare palms had a network of pores, larger than any he had ever seen, and through those pores he was able to sense the flavors and odors of everything surrounding him. It was a good thing, too, because evolution had forgotten to give the Hawkhorns nostrils and nasal passages.

His ears were small and pointed, barely up to human standards, far short of the hearing abilities he had possessed as a Firefly. And much to his regret, the night vision was gone. This slowed him considerably, since despite his enormous strength and armored body, he was unwilling to encounter any of the jungle's beasts of prey unless he could see them.

He was totally carnivorous. Beatrice Ngoni had told him that, but he hadn't wanted to kill the small animals he encountered and eat their raw flesh, so he had eaten some fruit instead, and had become immediately, violently sick to his stomach. It was possible, of course, that that particular fruit was poison, and that some other fruit would satisfy him, but he decided after the one experience to take Ngoni at her word. When he recovered he pulped a small, unsuspecting bird with his fist and ate it, skin, feathers, bones, and all—and had to admit that it compared favorably with the finest gourmet meals he had enjoyed as a Man.

The most unique feature of his new anatomy was the long, ridged, curving horn that sprang out of his forehead. When he had first seen the holographs of it, he was certain that it was used in battle, probably over females of the race, but he was wrong. Ngoni called it, for lack of a better term, a Horn of Perception, and that was precisely what it was: a unique empathic receiving station that read the emotions of all living things.

At first he thought that all it meant was that he would know which Hawkhorns liked him and which didn't, but he hadn't begun to suspect the ramifications of the Horn. When he killed the bird, he felt its terror and pain. When he plucked the fruit he had eaten from its branch, he sensed a very faint but real reaction, not of death, but an alien, almost incomprehensible, form of outrage and pain.

How the hell do they stand it? To keep these bodies going, they've got to make at least one kill a day. Don't the death throes of their prey drive them crazy?

On the other hand, they can't lie, because the Horn

would give them away immediately. And by the same token, I don't imagine they go to war very often, if at all. I barely sensed the fruit, and I was so hungry I ignored the bird—but how do you lock out the suffering of a thousand dying members of your own race?

The returning Pioneers had reported that the color patterns of the Hawkhorns' feathers seemed to indicate clans and tribes, and that possessors of one pattern tended to stay together. They occasionally found a lone Hawkhorn, but they never saw a Hawkhorn of one color pattern living with Hawkhorns of another. The clans themselves were seminomadic, moving from day to day as their domestic meat animals sought out better grazing, but always staying within well-defined borders.

This complicated Lennox's job. It wouldn't do to find *any* Hawkhorns; he had to find the *right* clan of Hawkhorns. Those that captured the four Pioneers had colors and patterns of feathers identical to his own, and he was sure that if he came upon a family with different colors, they would probably put him to death as an intruder, a spy, or simply an age-old blood enemy.

So he continued trudging through the seemingly endless rain forest, searching for signs of the Hawkhorns. It took him four days before he came upon one: a covered pit, obviously a trap for animals. His bushcraft was nil, so rather than try to follow the trail of those who had dug the trap, he remained in the vicinity of the pit, confident that somebody would soon be by to check on it.

He didn't have long to wait. Six hours later, just before twilight, a Hawkhorn—the first he had ever seen, other than himself—cautiously approached the pit. Its feather patterns were markedly different from Lennox's own—mostly reds and greens in small clusters against a tan background—and Lennox put enough stock in the Pioneers' observations that he decided not to openly approach the Hawkhorn.

He moved silently through the underbrush until he was about twenty feet away. The Hawkhorn was already showing signs of nervousness as its Horn picked up distinctly unfriendly emanations from Lennox. It straightened up abruptly, looked around, and then cautiously approached the pit.

It's not directional! That means he knows something's feeling violent emotions toward him, but he assumes they're coming from a captured animal in the pit.

The Hawkhorn would reach the pit in another two or three steps, and *then* it would know that the danger came from elsewhere. The thought galvanized Lennox into action, and he raced from the bushes and hurled himself into the small of the Hawkhorn's back before the being knew he was there. The Hawkhorn grunted in surprise and shot forward onto the thin grasses that covered the mouth of the pit, through them, and down some dozen feet to the pit's floor.

Lennox walked to the edge and looked down. The Hawkhorn, who seemed unharmed, got to its feet, brushed itself off, and peered up from the darkness within. Lennox's horn picked up sensations of hatred and dismay.

"Kill and be done," said the Hawkhorn in its deep, gravelly voice.

"I have no desire to kill you," responded Lennox. "I wish only to talk. If you give me the information I seek, I will help you out of the pit."

"Why should I believe a *droika*?" came the reply.

Since they were the same race, Lennox quickly concluded that *droika* referred to his color and pattern.

"You can believe me or you can stay there and starve to death," said Lennox. "It makes no difference to me."

The Hawkhorn continued staring up at him for a long minute, trying to make up its mind which of the two unpleasant choices was the less repugnant to it. At last it said, "I will talk."

"Good."

"Who are you?"

"My name is Lennox."

"That is not a *droika* name."

"It is now," said Lennox.

"What information do you seek?"

"The *droika* captured four aliens. Where can I find them?"

"I know nothing of that."

"All right, then. Where can I find the *droika*?"

The Hawkhorn stared at him. "How can you not know where your own clan is?"

"That is not your concern. Where can I find them?"

The Hawkhorn glared at him and made no response.

"All right," said Lennox with a shrug. "Starve and be damned."

He turned and began walking away from the pit. He was fully prepared to keep on walking and never look back, because he knew the being's Horn would be able to detect a ruse, and it was with a feeling of relief that he heard the harsh voice cry out when he was almost out of range:

"Come back! Help me out of this hole and I will take you to them!"

Lennox turned back and used his incredibly powerful new muscles to rip a ten-foot branch off a tree. He lowered it into the pit, then pulled it out while the Hawkhorn clung to it.

"What is your name?" he asked, when the Hawkhorn stood upon the ground once more.

"Yarlthop."

"How far away are we from the *droika*?"

"Not far. Perhaps a day, perhaps more."

"Then let us begin."

Yarlthop began walking through the forest, and Lennox fell into step behind him. It was an uneventful afternoon as the Hawkhorn continually chose the path of least resistance, but just before nightfall they spotted a small animal that resembled an extinct duiker of Earth more than any other beast to which Lennox could compare it. Yarlthop made a gesture for silence, then began moving off in a large semicircle around it. Lennox waited, motionless, until his Horn told him that the little animal had suddenly realized that there was danger nearby.

Lennox and the animal both heard the movement in the bushes to the left, but only Lennox realized that it was merely a rock that Yarlthop had thrown to distract it. A moment later he charged down upon the unsuspecting animal and clubbed it to death with a dead branch he had picked up during the stalk. This time Lennox not only felt the animal's fear and pain, but also Yarlthop's sense of triumph and his eagerness to get on with the feast.

Lennox realized that there was so much death going on around him all the time in the forest that he had become somewhat inured to it, for he found Yarlthop's emotional radiation to be far stronger than the wordless death agonies he was constantly receiving.

He joined the Hawkhorn at the carcass, helped rip the flesh apart, and gorged down almost five pounds of raw meat. They slept in the bole of an enormous tree that had been hollowed out and used as living quarters by some long-departed animal. Lennox assumed his Horn would let him know if Yarlthop tried to sneak off during the night, and when he woke up at daybreak he found the Hawkhorn sleeping peacefully next to him.

They were soon on the move again, making their way through the forest as it began to thin out a bit, and Lennox began sensing that Yarlthop was increasingly wary.

"What is the matter?" he asked.

"Soon we will be in the land of the *droika*," answered Yarlthop. "As soon as I am seen, they will kill me."

"I will tell them that you have done me a service, and that they must leave you alone."

The emotional radiation he picked up in response to his statement was so powerful and so confused that Lennox could only conclude that his answer was akin to stating that he was tired of walking and was going to take a moment to grow a set of wheels. He simply couldn't interpret the emotions he was receiving, but he got the distinct impression that the *droika* would sooner kill them both than let his companion live.

"Get me close to them, and you can leave," he said at last.

The Hawkhorn stared at him intently, trying to interpret the *lack* of radiation his own Horn was picking up. "What sort of *droika* are you?" he demanded.

"A very special one."

"That much is clear." Then, "We are already close to them."

"Closer," said Lennox.

Yarlthop commenced walking again, more cautiously this time, and within half an hour came to another halt.

"What is it now?" asked Lennox.

Yarlthop pointed to a tiny patch of color more than a mile away. *"Droika!"*

Lennox peered in the direction indicated, wishing that he still had his Firefly's vision. Finally he made out a few tiny yellow-orange-and-blue figures standing at the edge of a small field, watching perhaps three dozen cowlike creatures grazing.

"All right," said Lennox. "You have fulfilled your obligation. Go in peace."

Yarlthop stared at him in wonderment. "You really are not going to kill me!"

"You know I am not."

Or do you? Have the Hawkhorns learned to control their emotions to the point where they can't be read? He considered the possibility. *But that's ridiculous. I've read every response and every fear you've had since we met. So why are you surprised I'm keeping my word? Probably the thought of letting an enemy live is almost impossible to believe. Which means you probably do have wars after all—but for the life of me I don't understand how you can cause the suffering that entails when*

*it comes right back to you through your Horns. I still
have a lot to learn about you.*

"Would that all *droika* were like you," said Yarlthop, vanishing back into the depths of the forest.

*Now, what is that supposed to mean? That he wishes
they were like me because they're the bullies of the
planet, or because peace-loving Hawkhorns would be
easier to kill?*

Lennox continued to watch the *droika* for a few moments, trying to come up with a way to approach them,
when it finally occurred to him that he didn't *need* a
plan: he was every bit as much a *droika* as they were,
and since clans and tribes stuck together on Artismo, he
should be instantly accepted.

He began walking forward boldly, and had covered
almost half the distance between himself and the *droika*
before they spotted him. There were five of them, and
they clustered together as he neared them, speaking
among themselves.

When he got to within ten yards of them he came to a
halt.

*Do I greet them, or do they greet me? Is there some
symbol of rank I should recognize?*

He stood motionless, staring at them.

"You are not of our family," said the nearest of the
Hawkhorns.

Lennox's Horn sensed no anxiety. "No, I am not," he
answered.

"You must be far from home," said another. "If you
are hungry, we can slaughter a *boisha* for you."

"That is not necessary," said Lennox, who, although

hungry, had no desire to be hit with the emotional trauma from a dying meat animal.

"Have you encountered any *bedrona*? We are told that they have been seen deep in the forest."

What the hell is a bedrona*? An animal, or maybe a member of Yarlthop's clan?*

He was about to reply that he had seen nothing of interest, when it occurred to him that their own Horns would tell them he was lying.

Okay, then, let's assume they're talking about Yarlthop.

"Yes, I have."

"You are fortunate to have survived."

"Very."

"What is your name, wayfarer?"

"Lennox."

The Hawkhorn's face contorted into a frown. "That is a very unusual name."

"It is a harsh, angular sound," offered a second Hawkhorn. "More fitting to an alien than to a *droika*."

"I would not know," answered Lennox. "I have never seen an alien."

"And yet you tense at the thought of one," noted the Hawkhorn. "Where is your courage, Lennox?"

"I have a healthy respect for the unknown," answered Lennox carefully. "Perhaps if I ever see an alien, I will feel as you do."

"They are in Shumario's corral, if you really care to look at one," said the first Hawkhorn.

"They?" repeated Lennox. "You mean that you have captured more than one alien species?"

"One species, four aliens," was the answer.

"I would very much like to see them," said Lennox, trying to keep his excitement in check.

The five seemed uncomfortable with the strength of his emotional radiation. Two of them backed away a few feet, their feathered skins twitching.

"Well?" said the first Hawkhorn after a moment.

"Well what?" asked Lennox, confused.

"If you wish to see them, and have no duties to prevent you, then go."

Go? Go where?

"I have been alone a long time in the forest," said Lennox. "Perhaps one of you would like to accompany me."

"Why?" asked the Hawkhorn, honestly curious.

"I miss the companionship of my fellow *droika*."

More curiosity was radiated. "You do?"

"Yes."

"You are a most unusual *droika*. It is fitting that you have an unusual name."

"I will go with him," volunteered the smallest of the Hawkhorns.

"You just want to see your *ganshi*," said the first Hawkhorn, and all of them laughed.

Lennox instantly sensed the small Hawkhorn's embarrassment.

His girlfriend? His mother? His pet boisha?

"Come, Lennox," said the small Hawkhorn. "We do not need to linger in the presence of these *bijuna*."

Lennox sensed anger, then good humor. Obviously it was an insult under some circumstances, but the others instantly recognized it as a good-natured comeback.

"Take one of the *boisha* with you," said the first Hawkhorn.

"Some of us are not too old and lazy to catch our own meals," was the response.

"Remember that when your bellies are empty."

There was a little more banter and then Lennox and the Hawkhorn headed off in a northerly direction. Lennox was filled with questions—the Republic knew even less about the Hawkhorns than they had known about the Fireflies—but he didn't dare ask. If he showed too much ignorance, he couldn't lie or bluster his way out of it, not when this race possessed these remarkable Horns. He settled for observing the foliage, trying to categorize the trees and shrubs and flowers and grasses.

His guide's name was Elormi, and he was very sensitive about his size. Lennox had thought he might be a youth, but he was an adult, and to prove his worth in this very physical society he was always volunteering for the most strenuous and dangerous tasks, doubtless the reason he had agreed to lead Lennox to the Pioneer Corps prisoners.

Elormi seemed as willing to walk in silence as Lennox was, and the day passed uneventfully. In late afternoon Elormi quickly manufactured a primitive sling from a very flexible vine, found a stone, and killed a small rodentlike animal from a safe distance—safe not from attack by the little animal, but safe from its emotional radiations. They ate it raw, and Lennox marveled once again at the remarkable job Beatrice Ngoni's staff had done on his taste buds and his digestive system.

"Tomorrow morning we will arrive at Shumario's

corral,'' announced Elormi after they had finished eating, ''and there we shall part.''

''I appreciate your having come with me,'' said Lennox.

''How do you plan to rescue them?''

Lennox started in surprise.

''Rescue *who*?'' he asked.

''The aliens.''

''What makes you think I have any interest in rescuing them at all?''

''That is why you are here, is it not?''

Lennox, who realized that Elormi would instantly know if he lied, elected to offer no answer at all.

''I have been with you all day,'' continued Elormi, ''and I know that whatever else you are, you are not a *droika,* despite your appearance.''

''Why have you not attempted to kill me, then?'' asked Lennox.

''Because I can read no hostility within you.''

''Even so, they are *droika* prisoners. Why wouldn't you try to stop me?''

''Because the rage and aggression emanating from the prisoners is corrupting everyone around them. I think it is better for us that they leave.''

''Will you help me, then?''

''If you will do me a favor in return.''

''What is it?''

''The prisoners come from another world, do they not?''

''They do.''

''Are there many other worlds?''

''More than you can count,'' said Lennox.

"My father is a storyteller, as was his father before him, and *his* father before *him*. Someday, when I am too old to tend the *boisha* or do my other duties, I will be a storyteller, too."

Lennox stared at him, puzzled. "What has that got to do with—"

"The stories that my father and grandfather tell never change," continued Elormi. "I should like to find new stories to tell. I want to visit other worlds, and come back to charge the imaginations of my people with wonders they have never imagined." He paused. "That is my offer. I will help you, if you will help me."

I'll be damned! A feathered, horned mythmaker living naked on an alien world!

"Elormi," said Lennox, "you've got yourself a bargain."

TWENTY-ONE

Lennox trudged through the swamp, marveling at the way his feet contracted as he pulled them up out of the muck. The morning rain pelted him, but was unable to get through his feathers to reach his skin.

They had walked most of the night, and now he could see what he assumed was Shumario's corral in a clearing up ahead. It was perhaps eight feet tall and fenced with crude upright boards, so he was unable to see what lay within.

"It's a big compound for just four Men," he remarked as he and Elormi paused to survey it from more than a mile away.

"What are Men?" asked Elormi.

"That's what the aliens call themselves."

"Ah." A brief pause. "There are a number of *boisha* in it, too."

"What about guards?"

"A few."

"How few?" asked Lennox.

"What difference does it make? We are *droika*. They won't bother us."

"They will once we take the prisoners away."

"They won't even know they're gone."

Lennox wished he could frown, because it was a puzzling statement, but he merely remained silent and continued looking at the corral. It was almost four hundred yards long and perhaps half that wide, easily capable of holding a couple of thousand *boisha*. Probably they would all be taken out to graze as soon as the rain stopped. He scanned the area, again cursing the vision Beatrice Ngoni's team had given him, and looked for Hawkhorns. As far as he could tell, there were none to be seen.

"Where *is* everybody?" he asked.

"Most will remain sheltered until the rain stops," answered Elormi. "A few are guarding the prisoners. Some may even have taken their animals out of the corral to graze."

"Shumario doesn't own all the animals?"

"Shumario owns the corral."

"So everyone puts their animals in the corral at night for safety?"

"Of course."

Lennox looked behind him. The forest began no more than one hundred yards away. Still, the distance from the corral to the forest was a long way for the Pioneers to walk without being spotted.

Elormi looked up at the sky. "We had better hurry,"

he said. "I don't think the rain will last more than another hour."

He began walking toward the corral, followed by Lennox, who still had no idea how to get the prisoners out without first confronting the guards. As they walked across the swamp, their feet made loud sucking sounds, but there was no one around to hear. The ground became firmer as they neared the corral, and they stopped when they were about twenty yards away.

"Now what?" asked Lennox.

"Now we locate the prisoners."

"How?"

Elormi gave him a look of utter disbelief, and held both of his hands up, palms facing the fence. Puzzled, Lennox did the same—and suddenly the odor of animals and excrement came to him.

Of course! I'd forgotten all about the pores in my hands!

He began walking down the wall, his sensitive palms analyzing all the many odors, and finally he came to one that he had not experienced since leaving the hospital. It was so strange, so totally out of place, that even if he had not encountered it before he would have known it belonged to the Men.

Elormi had also stopped moving, as if he, too, had encountered the odor and knew it could belong to nothing else.

Lennox knew that his next step would reveal he could speak Man's language. He stared at Elormi, wondering how the little Hawkhorn would react to it. Would he feel like a traitor to his race, or was his desire to see other worlds and learn other myths so great that it wouldn't bother him? After a moment Lennox realized that it made no difference, that if he was going to get the Men to safety before the rains stopped and the Hawkhorns came out to get their cattle, he was going to have to do it *now*.

"Hello," he said in Terran, his tongue and lips mangling the pronunciation, but not beyond the ability to make himself understood. "This is Xavier William Lennox. I've come to rescue you."

He didn't have to wait for the reply. His Horn told him that he had just produced a condition of hope and extreme excitement in four different entitics.

"Thank God you've come!" said a feminine voice. "This is Pioneer Elaine Joubert!"

"Are you all healthy enough to walk a mile within the next half hour?" asked Lennox.

"Three of us are. Robert Johannsen has come down with some sort of fever. He's too weak to walk at all."

"No problem," said Lennox. "I can carry him. How close are your guards?"

"They're on the other side of the corral, where there's shelter from the rain."

"Can they see you?"

"At this moment, yes."

"What do you mean, 'at this moment'?"

"When the animals get between us, their view is blocked."

"All right. Wait until the animals block them again and then let me know. And stand a few feet back from the wall of the corral."

The signal came about three minutes later, and Lennox folded his thick fingers into a huge fist and drove it into the wall with all the enormous strength his new body possessed. It went right through the board. He punched through two more boards, and then he and Elormi quickly pulled the fragments out.

An auburn-haired woman stepped halfway through the opening he had created, then froze when she saw the two Hawkhorns confronting her.

"It's all right," said Lennox, still speaking in Terran. "I'll explain later. We're friends."

She paused for another instant, then quickly stepped through, followed by two other women. Lennox entered the corral, found an emaciated man lying in the rain, his body burning with fever, and lifted him up over a broad, feathered shoulder. Then he rejoined the others.

"Our destination is the edge of that forest," he said, pointing toward the trees. "Don't try to run; no one will see us until the rain stops. Walk very carefully through the swamp. The only way we'll get caught is if you get mired down often enough along the way."

It took the three humans almost an hour to negotiate the swamp that Lennox and Elormi had crossed in ten minutes, but eventually they passed through it and were a half mile into the jungle when the rain finally subsided.

"Who are you really, and how did you learn our language?" asked Elaine Joubert when they stopped to rest.

"I'll explain it all tonight," said Lennox. "Just catch your breath now and let me know when you're ready to walk again. We've got to get a lot deeper into the forest before we're safe."

"Then what?" she asked.

"There's a ship due to pick us up in a week. We'll reach the contact point in about five days."

"What if it had taken you longer to rescue us?"

"It might well have," replied Lennox. "The ship is scheduled to scan the area once a week for four months, after which there would very likely have been a military invasion. You four would doubtless have been killed before your captors surrendered. Then the Republic would have declared you heroes and erected statues to you and bragged about their great victory over this technologically advanced civilization."

Lennox turned his attention to Robert Johannsen. His Horn detected no pain, but rather a total lack of interest in remaining alive. Even if he'd been slender to begin with, the man had obviously lost an enormous amount of weight—and despite the abundance of water on the planet he was in a state of severe dehydration. The three other Pioneers had done what they could for him, but with no medicine, no shelter, and very little hygiene, they'd barely been able to keep him alive.

Lennox coaxed some water between Johannsen's lips, then lifted him gently to his shoulder and announced that it was time to start walking again.

They marched through the forest for the next three days, and on the fourth morning Lennox summoned the Pioneers and Elormi to his side.

"If we keep marching at this pace, Johannsen is going to die before we reach the pickup point," he announced.

"Then we'll slow our pace and the ship can pick us up a week later," said Elaine.

Lennox shook his massive head. "No," he said. "There's every likelihood that we're being tracked by your captors. If we slow down they're sure to catch up with us.''

"Then what do you suggest?'' she asked. ''We can't just leave him here.''

"I'll stay behind with him,'' said Lennox. ''I'll give the landing coordinates to Elormi, and he will lead the three of you to the spot. And remember: I've promised him that he could go with you. He speaks no Terran, but someone in the Department of Alien Affairs can transmit a Hawkhorn language tape to wherever he decides to go.''

"We can't just leave you behind like that!'' she protested.

"My job was to rescue you and get you back to a Republic world.''

"But the Hawkhorns will track you down!''

"Not a chance,'' said Lennox. ''I can move much faster without you. Just tell the ship to come back each week. When Johannsen's finally healthy enough, we'll be there to meet it.''

"Are you sure . . . ?''

"Believe me, we'll be safer without you than with you.''

She stared at him, then reluctantly nodded her head. ''All right. If you say so.''

"I do. Now just wait a moment while I explain the situation to Elormi.''

He turned to the little Hawkhorn. ''You're taking them to the landing place. I'm going to stay behind.''

"I don't know what you told them,'' replied Elormi, ''but I cannot understand why they believed you.''

"They are not gifted with the Horn,'' said Lennox.

"Why are you staying behind?"

"I have my reasons. Will you guide them as I ask?"

"Yes. Do they know I am to accompany them on your ship?"

"They know."

Elormi stood up. "Then we shall leave now."

"Thank you for your help, Elormi," said Lennox, also getting to his feet. "Watch out for *bedrona* in the woods; I ran into one on my way here." He paused. "Good-bye, and good luck."

"I shall bring back stories to stir the imaginations of all my people," said Elormi. He headed off, and the three healthy Pioneers followed him.

Lennox remained standing until they were out of sight, then sat down again beside the dying Johannsen. His Horn told him that it would be two hours, three at most, before the man gave up the ghost.

He broke a branch off a tree, shaped it as best he could with his powerful, double-thumbed hands, and began digging a grave. He completed it about ten minutes before Johannsen died. He then placed the withered corpse into the hole, covered it with mud, and arranged two small twigs in a tiny cross that would not attract any attention if the *droika* were actually following him, which he doubted.

In fact, he had every intention of joining the *droika* in a few days and learning what he could about their society. After all, he hadn't undergone the months of surgery and adjustment just to get four people he couldn't care less about out of captivity. It would be more than three months before the Republic gave up on him; he could spend the next ten or eleven weeks becoming a *droika*.

But first he had a body to field-test.

He used the sense organs in the palms of his hands to hunt down a small animal, caught it when it ran into the mud and got stuck, and calmly examined its emotions as he killed it. It still bothered him, this overwhelming sensation of terror and pain that his victims emitted, but there were ways of adjusting to it. The Hawkhorns had, and now that he was one of them, he would, too.

That night he built a small fire. Not to cook his meal, which he had eaten raw, nor to keep warm, for his feathers and his armored skin protected him from the elements. It was more in the nature of an experiment, as Xavier William Lennox, who had once been a Man, coldly and dispassionately studied the agonized sensations of the green wood as it was consumed by flame.

TWENTY-TWO

Nora Wallace looked up from her desk and saw the well-dressed woman standing in front of her.

"Can I help you?" she said politely.

"I'm here to stop you from destroying Xavier Lennox," replied Angela Stone, trying to keep her emotions in check.

"You must be . . ."

"His agent."

"I was about to say, his ex-wife."

"That, too."

"I've tried to contact him a number of times since he returned from Artismo," offered Nora, "but he refuses to answer the messages I've left."

"What are you planning to do?" demanded Angela bitterly. "Turn him into yet another monster?"

"That's *his* choice," said Nora. "You're very distressed, Miss Stone. Won't you please sit down?"

Angela sat in the chair Nora had indicated and glared at her. When it became apparent that Nora was not going to speak first, she said, "He's not human anymore!"

"Of course not. He's a Hawkhorn."

Angela shook her head. "You don't understand."

"Then perhaps you can enlighten me," said Nora.

"He was different the last time he came back, when he was a Firefly. He was depressed, he moped around the house, he was uncommunicative, but he was still a human being under that exterior."

"And you feel he's not anymore?"

"He used to be a voracious reader," said Angela. She paused, her face and voice deeply troubled. "He gave all his books and tapes away the week he got back from Artismo."

"Perhaps he has new interests," suggested Nora.

"He has. He got rid of his chemical dryshower and replaced it with one that uses real water. Now he spends ten to twelve hours a day standing under the water. Just standing there. Not washing, not singing, not doing anything."

"His new body was created for a world where it rains most of the time," explained Nora. "If that's the only problem . . ."

"Hardly!" interrupted Angela. "I just bailed him out of jail!"

Nora Wallace frowned. "Oh?"

"He has a neighbor who imported two cats from Earth about a year ago. One of the cats just had kittens."

She paused, again trying to control her emotions. "The police arrested him after he killed and ate all the kittens and their mother!"

"He did *what*?"

"You heard me! He's not Xavier anymore! When he's not in the shower or killing small, defenseless animals, he just sits. He never speaks, never answers. He used to love music. Now he refuses to listen to it."

"Has he done any work at all?" asked Nora.

"None."

"Has he discussed any of his experiences on Artismo with you?"

Angela shook her head. "I've asked, but he just says I wouldn't be able to comprehend what he was talking about." She made an effort to mask her fear. "I believe him. Lord knows I can't comprehend anything else about him!"

"I sympathize, Miss Stone," said Nora. "But I don't know what you expect *me* to do about it."

"Change him back into a Man. And get him some psychiatric help, someone who can reach the real Xavier Lennox while some tiny part of him is still there to reach."

"He's a creature of free will, like you and me," replied Nora. "I can't force him to become a Man again if he doesn't want to."

"He's a creature, all right," said Angela, "but *not* like you and me. I saw him watching a small child through the window the other day. It scared the hell out of me. He looked . . . *hungry*!" She paused and then glared across the desk at Nora. "You were the one who arranged for him to change shapes in the first place. You've got to make him change back.''

"It's not up to me," replied Nora gently. "It's *his* decision."

"He's not capable of making a rational decision."

"Maybe he's more rational than you think. He performed both of his missions superbly."

"I don't *care* about your goddamned missions!" snapped Angela. "I care about Xavier!"

"He saved four human beings at serious risk to himself while he was on Artismo," said Nora. "Does that sound like an alien to you?"

"He wants to kill and eat children, and you're talking about him like he's some kind of hero!" Angela paused, making an almost physical effort to control her emotions. "You don't know him like I do. I lived with him for three years, and one of the reasons I left him is because he is one of the most self-centered men I've ever met. I tell you that, for all his many virtues, the *real* Xavier wouldn't go one step out of his way to help another human being unless he thought there was a book or a story in it."

"Perhaps there is."

"As soon as he got home, he instructed me to buy him out of his writing contracts, whatever it cost."

"Did you?"

"No. Once you change him back into a Man, it's the only way he'll be able to make a living."

"You told him that?"

"No. I didn't want a knock-down drag-out fight. He could break me in half with that new body of his, and who knows what his mental processes are like?"

"So you told him you bought him out of the contracts?"

"Yes."

"He knew you were lying, Miss Stone."

"I doubt it."

"I'm sure you are a fine liar—no offense intended—but he has certain abilities as a Hawkhorn. Believe me when I tell you that you cannot hide the truth from him, any more than you can hide your emotions."

"He can read my mind?"

"Not exactly. But he can read your emotions, and since he's very intelligent, he can doubtless deduce what you are thinking."

"That's obscene! To have your mind stripped naked in front of this alien *thing* . . ."

"He's not a thing, Miss Stone," said Nora. "He's simply a Man who's wearing a costume, playing out a role for which he was intensely schooled. He just hasn't realized that he's no longer onstage."

"You have an answer for everything!" snapped Angela. "But my husband is vanishing into this costume you've created for him, and you don't seem to understand what's happening."

"Your *ex*-husband," Nora corrected her. "You have to let go, Miss Stone. Whether he chooses to become a Man again or not, he will never be the Xavier Lennox you knew again."

"Husband, ex-husband, what's the difference? A very unique, very talented man may even now be beyond your help, and you won't even acknowledge that a problem exists!"

"That's neither true nor fair, Miss Stone," said Nora.

"There is no precedent for this situation. No other Man has ever undergone what Xavier Lennox has undergone. None has ever had to return from it." She paused and looked across the desk, not without compassion, at the troubled woman confronting her. "We're in virgin territory here. I have no more idea where it's leading him than you do."

"And while you're pontificating, he's torturing and eating small animals and spending half his life under streams of steaming water," concluded Angela bitterly.

"I'll go this far, Miss Stone," said Nora, measuring each word carefully. "I will insist that he be brought here immediately for psychiatric testing, and should the tests confirm your fears, he will not be allowed to interact with any Men until he is cured. Will that be acceptable to you?"

"And you'll physically change him back into what he was?"

"I can't promise that," said Nora. "It's still *his* decision." She paused again. "But if our psychiatric staff says he's ready, it shouldn't be a problem."

Angela got to her feet and walked to the door, then turned and glared at the pudgy woman sitting at the desk.

"You broke him. You fix him."

Then she was gone, and Nora Wallace was immediately on the vidphone, speaking to one of her subordinates.

"It's time to bring our Mister Lennox in, whether he wants to come or not," she said. "Put him in isolation until the psych people can run their tests on him. No visitors.''

"Not even Miss Stone?"

"*Especially* not Miss Stone."

TWENTY-THREE

❧❧❧❧❧❧❧❧❧❧❧

Good morning, Mister Lennox,'' said Nora Wallace, entering the small hospital room. "How are we today?"

Lennox stared at her, but made no reply.

"I just heard from your agent again. Would you like me to start putting her calls through?"

Lennox continued staring silently.

"Really, Mister Lennox, if you do not answer me, I won't know what to tell her."

"Tell her to leave me alone," said Lennox in his incredibly deep voice. The words were mispronounced but understandable.

"As you wish." She paused. "And I really must ask you to stop playing games with our psychiatric staff."

No reply.

"One of them thinks you're a homicidal maniac. Another finds you perfectly normal in all respects. The third thinks you're a manic depressive with shadings of paranoia. Two others find you so far off the scale that they don't know how to evaluate you.''

"They're all fools," said Lennox.

"Yes, probably. But did you really have to answer them in the language of the Hawkhorns? It took an extra week to translate everything you said."

"I'm a Hawkhorn. It's my language."

"But you are speaking Terran with me. Why?"

No answer.

"It wouldn't be because you want something from me, would it?" continued Nora.

"You know what I want."

"Well, I think we both know what you *don't* want," said Nora. "There are times, however, when I think that even *you* don't quite know what you want."

"I won't be a Man again," said Lennox. "There's too much out there."

"I beg your pardon?"

"Too much to become, too much to learn."

"Will all this knowledge die with you, or do you intend to codify it and pass it on at some point in the future?"

"I've been thoroughly debriefed. They've sucked all the knowledge out of me." Lennox paused. "Besides, you don't give a damn if it dies with me or not."

"Certainly I do."

"You can do a lot of things to me, but lying isn't one of them."

"The dissemination of your knowledge is not one of my priorities," admitted Nora. "But I *do* care."

Lennox made no reply.

"Come now, Mister Lennox," said Nora. "If you want to leave this room, you must cooperate with me."

Lennox emitted a hollow, hooting noise that sounded just vaguely like an alien laugh.

"You think you can keep me here one second longer than I'm willing to be kept?"

He swung a massive arm against the wall, and put an enormous hole in it.

"I'm going to have to bill you for repairs," noted Nora.

"Get on with it."

"With the billing?"

"You know what I want."

"Yes, I do . . . but I don't know if you're capable of handling it. You've changed considerably since your first surgery."

"Of course I have!" shouted Lennox, and the volume alone caused her to jump back. "I've read the innermost feeling of every living thing on Artismo. I've felt the death throes of leaves, the panic of prey trying to fight off their predators. I've felt the ecstasy of two Hawkhorns engaging in sex, and I've even experienced the massive outrage of a baby being born. How could I *not* have changed?"

"I understand."

"I doubt it." Lennox glared hostilely at her. "I won't go back to being a Man."

"I honestly don't think I could get permission for the surgery," she said bluntly. "Too many of your reactions and opinions are no longer human. For better or worse, we seem to be stuck with you, and you with us."

Suddenly she smiled. "By the way, it might interest you to know that we fired the psychiatrist who said you were normal."

"The little one? Skinny, with blond-gray hair?"

"That's the one."

"I should have eaten him when I had the chance."

"It's comments like that that do not endear you to the rest of the staff," she noted mildly. "We're running out of orderlies to attend to your needs."

"Then let's do the surgery and get it over with."

"It's not that simple," said Nora. "According to Doctor Ngoni, every time you undergo a body-altering operation, they make so many changes and adjustments that it limits what can be done the next time."

He stared at her questioningly.

"You can only handle two or three more operations," continued Nora. "Then you have to go back to being a Man, or stay what you've become. As it is, we're limited in what we can do with you now. There's a chlorine world we'd love to send you to, but Doctor Ngoni, for all her skills, cannot turn you into a chlorine breather. Nor, by the same token, can we alter you and set you down on a frigid methane world." She paused. "In fact, at the moment, there is only one world where we both require your services and can actually arrange to have them."

"Then that's where I'm going."

"Don't be too hasty, Mister Lennox," she said. "Your mission this time would be very different from your last two."

"So what?"

"I'm trying to explain to you that if you undergo the

operation and we set you down on Tamerlaine, you may spend the next year as the only sentient being on the planet. It could be very lonely, frustrating work.''

''What about the race I'll be impersonating?''

''Well, therein lies our problem. . . .''

TWENTY-FOUR

※※※※※※※※※※※※※※

Tamerlaine was an interesting world. More to the point, it was a valuable one.

Man was in the process of moving his headquarters from Earth, which was isolated out on the Spiral Arm of the galaxy, to huge Deluros VIII, which was more centrally located. It was from Deluros and its neighboring worlds that Man's expansion into the galaxy truly began. The Republic began assimilating nearby worlds, then expanding farther and farther in two directions: the Outer Frontier, those distant worlds out on the Galactic Rim, and the Inner Frontier, those worlds near the Galactic Core.

It was the duty of the Department of Cartology not merely to map the galaxy and the worlds therein, but also to plan the grand strategy for the Republic's expansion. Usually these lines of expansion followed clearly discernible patterns, based on trading routes and potential armed opposition, but every now and then the Pioneer Corps found a world well off the beaten path that Cartography felt was worth exploiting.

Such a world was Tamerlaine, a small planet circling a nondescript G-type star deep in the Inner Frontier. For Tamerlaine possessed abundant fissionable materials, and these materials were indispensable to the Republic.

A century or two earlier, the Republic would have just moved in and taken what it wanted, but as more and more intelligent races were assimilated, Man became very conscious of his image. He may have been the single most powerful race in the galaxy at this point in time, but he was outnumbered hundreds to one, and these days he used force only as a last resort.

If Tamerlaine was devoid of sentient life, there was nothing to stop the Republic from staking a claim and plundering its resources. If sentient life existed, then it became a matter for the Department of Alien Affairs and its Diplomatic Corps, and only if they failed to reach an accommodation would the military be brought in on some pretext or another.

But after three years of careful observation, the Department's best alien psychologists had been unable to determine whether the highest native life-form on Tamerlaine was sentient or not. And without that knowledge, the various branches of the Department and indeed the entire government of the Republic began arguing so furiously and at such cross purposes that all plans concerning Tamerlaine were put on hold until it was conclusively shown whether or not the planet was inhabited by sentient beings.

Finally, the entire affair was handed over to Nora Wallace. Her first step was to capture and sacrifice three of the inhabitants in question, and turn them over to Beatrice Ngoni and her staff. When it was determined that they could turn Lennox into a Wheeler, as the beings were dubbed, she quickly obtained the necessary funding because of Lennox's previous successes and gave the order to proceed.

That had been four months ago.

This time the various surgical procedures took a little longer, but the period of training was virtually nil. As a Wheeler, Lennox had no powers of speech, so there was no language to learn. No one knew if the Wheelers were sentient, so there was no culture to study. His physical abilities, while unusual, were not difficult to master, so only two weeks were spent mastering his new body and learning its limitations. Then he was set down on Tamerlaine, told that he would be picked up in six months, and urged to protect himself and the Republic's massive investment in his new body.

He had no eyes with which to survey his surroundings, nor legs with which to walk through them. Though a carnivore, he had no hands with which to grab his prey, no claws with which to rend its flesh, no vocal chords with which to roar and frighten it into submission.

He had a long blue tongue that could extend more than fifteen inches out of his mouth. It sensed light and patterns and movement, and caught the slightest odors that wafted to him on the mild breeze. He had a new organ grafted onto the middle of his sleek muzzle; it saw and identified the weak electrical forces that were emitted by living things.

His body was covered by layers of fat and a rough, almost impervious epidermis. At rest he resembled nothing more than a giant tan slug, but when he rolled himself into a ball and pushed off with the dozens of tiny pseudo-toes that lined both sides of it, he was capable of rolling at speeds of up to twenty miles an hour.

He found himself in a large, flat field. The mosslike vegetation beneath him felt somehow *right,* as if it had been made especially for his comfort when rolling. Somehow he knew that it was a pale yellow-green, though he had no eyes to see it. Off in the distance were hundreds of tall, slender trees, some of them reaching up two hundred feet and more to the bright blue sky. He suddenly realized that he was hungry, and so he decided to test his locomotion skills and rolled across the field toward the trees.

He sensed that he wasn't keeping a straight line, and began experimenting, as he had at the hospital, pushing out with his right-side pseudo-toes while curling his left ones beneath him and burying them in his rolls of fat. Now he veered too much to the left, and he adjusted by bringing his left toes into play. It took a few minutes, but finally he got the hang of it. Then he experimented with different speeds, and with stopping and starting. When he felt confident in his locomotive skills, he left the field and headed into the trees.

He found two trees that were about three feet apart, willed the flap atop his tongue to open, and began spraying out the sticky, translucent material that would form his web. Back and forth between the trees he sprayed, stringing line after line of the substance. It didn't seem too secure to him, so he then began spraying up and down, forming a web of perhaps three hundred tiny squares, beginning two inches off the ground and reaching a height of almost three feet.

Then, because some instinct told him that the likelihood of that particular web producing immediate results was minimal, he sprayed a dozen more webs at regular intervals, until he had covered more than an acre.

This done, he rolled on through the trees, searching for other Wheelers. He was aware of the chirping of avians, the snorting of small rodentlike animals, the tiny scraping noises of insects burrowing beneath the ground. The scent of distant water came to his tongue, but his new body had no need for it; he would get all the moisture he needed from the innards of his kills.

He began backtracking after a few minutes, because he didn't want to get too far from his webs, and he hadn't been given any kind of a homing instinct. He checked them all out, found nothing there, and realized that the sun was starting to dip low in the sky.

He had been told that Wheelers were the top of the food chain on Tamerlaine, but he decided not to believe it until he knew the planet better, and he began searching for shelter for the night. He found the hollowed-out trunk of a tree, wedged his body into it, and did his best to ignore his hunger pangs as he settled in for the night.

He felt frustrated. He'd made contact with the Fireflies less than three hours after landing on Medina, and he'd come across a Hawkhorn by the end of his first day on Artismo. But here, on Tamerlaine, not only hadn't he made any contact, but he still hadn't the slightest idea what to do if he *did* make contact with another Wheeler. And in the meantime, he was going hungry in a forest that his new senses told him was virtually overflowing with prey.

He awoke to the sound of avians singing, realized that he had spent the entire night unmolested, undulated out from his tree trunk, and made the rounds of his webs again.

Nothing. Not even an insect.

He rolled through the forest, a little farther this time than the previous day, seeking other Wheelers. There weren't any. He returned every two or three hours to determine whether his webs had finally captured anything. They hadn't. He created another dozen webs during the course of the day.

He made a final web-checking excursion at twilight with no success. Since he also hadn't come across any sign of predators, large or small, he elected not to spend the night scrunched uncomfortably inside the tree trunk, but fell asleep right next to it.

He awoke a few minutes before dawn, ravenously hungry. He checked his webs again, and again they were empty.

The situation had passed from annoying to desperate, and he made up his mind to leave the area and go where there was hopefully better hunting. He proceeded due west for almost two hours when he came to a web of such intricacy that it actually struck him as a work of art. There were delicate patterns, subtle curves and angles, forming a tapestry of almost hypnotic geometric patterns.

Ten yards farther he came to a second, similarly intricate, web, and in this one a small avian was struggling to free itself. Lennox pounced on the avian, killing it with a single bite and swallowing it with three more.

It didn't quite satisfy his appetite, but he knew that it would hold him for the rest of the day if he couldn't catch his own meal. He was still studying the web, wondering if there was something about the pattern that had attracted the avian, when a burly round body bore down upon him and hurled itself onto his back.

Because he wasn't curled into a ball at the time, Lennox found himself flattened out on the moss, while the Wheeler that had attacked him rolled over him, circled around, and charged him again, this time from the front. Lennox rolled over, barely avoiding the Wheeler, then formed a sphere and rolled about twenty yards away.

When he wasn't pursued he stopped, turned, and faced his attacker. It was a Wheeler of approximately his own size and weight, and it showed no desire to chase him. It shifted its weight from right to left, swaying slightly, its tongue extended in his direction, observing him as surely as if it had had eyes.

Lennox wanted to explain to the Wheeler that he meant no harm, that he had simply taken the animal because he was weak from hunger—but he didn't know how to communicate with it.

When it made no aggressive motion toward him, he rolled a couple of feet closer to it. Suddenly the Wheeler seemed to tense, to compress its body into a tighter ball. Lennox took it as a warning, and stopped moving.

The two of them remained thus for almost an hour. Every time Lennox approached—and now he did it by inches rather than feet—the Wheeler tensed and prepared to attack him. Every time he retreated the Wheeler relaxed. When it became apparent that the Wheeler wasn't about to leave its web, that in fact Lennox had invaded its territory, Lennox finally decided to leave.

He had no idea how to get back to his own webs, nor did he care to. He obviously needed to cast webs of far more intricacy anyway, and so he continued on his way. About half a mile farther he came to some more webs, different in pattern from the ones he had just left behind, but all very similar to each other, and concluded that he had wandered onto another Wheeler's home turf. A small rodent struggled weakly in one of the nets, and Lennox waited until dark before approaching and eating it. He half-expected to be attacked in the process, but nothing happened, and when he was done he left, breaking through a couple of webs in the darkness.

The next morning he found an unclaimed area of about three hundred yards on a side, and began creating his webs. He didn't know exactly what kind of design attracted what kind of animal, but he knew that the successful ones had been far more complex than his earlier attempts. He began by creating a large rectangle, placing a cross within it, and then, radiating out from the very center of the cross, he did his best to create a complex pattern. He wasn't as skilled as he might have wished, but when he was finished he rolled back a few feet and considered it both as a trap and a work of art. He hoped it worked better as a trap.

He spent the rest of the day creating half a dozen more webs, then went to sleep on the mosslike vegetation next to the last of them.

When he woke up and made his rounds, he found that his webs were all empty.

As he tried to figure out what he had done wrong, it occurred to him that he might starve before he found out if the Wheelers were sentient.

TWENTY-FIVE

Lennox set out once again to explore his new world.
Twice during the morning he chanced upon other
Wheelers. In neither instance did they seem hostile—
but then, in neither instance did he try to steal food from
them. Both observed him carefully while working on
their webs, but neither made any attempt to approach
him or chase him away.

Then, just when he had decided that the Wheelers
were a solitary, territorial race, he came across three of
them stringing webs in concert. All three were within a
few feet of each other, and seemed to be working har-
moniously. Each was constantly inspecting the others'
webs, then going back to work on its own.

So they weren't solitary after all. Lennox approached
them cautiously, and all three stopped working and
turned to face him. He wanted to explain that he came in

peace, but of course he had no vocal chords, so he merely rolled up to within a few feet of the nearest and stopped, ready to run—or roll—for his life in the case of a sudden attack.

The Wheelers watched him intently for the better part of five minutes, and then, one by one, they went back to their web-making and ignored him. He approached still closer, but none of them paid him any attention.

Finally, unable to think of what to do next, he decided to leave. He turned and began rolling through the woods, trying to make sense out of what he had seen. Did they communicate? If so, how? And was it *sentient* communication, or simply a banding together of three Wheelers who had been having as hard a time catching food as he himself had been having, and had decided to pool their resources? If so, was *that* a sign of sentience?

He assumed that the only thing likely to precipitate an attack would be to rob another Wheeler of its prey—but that didn't make life any easier for him. Until he learned to spin more intricate webs, he was going to *have* to scavenge off existing webs. Furthermore, the attack itself wasn't necessarily a sign of sentience; everything from insects to the largest predators protected their territories and stopped intruders from plundering their kills.

Still, if Wheelers were territorial, how had the three of them gotten together? He'd been given every sensory organ a Wheeler had, and he couldn't find any organ that would allow him to communicate with them. He couldn't even change facial expressions. So how did they know to come together, those three? What instinct convinced them that three Wheelers working in concert could catch more prey than three Wheelers working alone—and how did they know in *which* Wheeler's territory they were supposed to spin their webs? Had one of them summoned the other two? And if so, how?

Lennox pondered the questions for the better part of the day as he wandered aimlessly through the woods. He paid no attention to where he was going, so wrapped up was he in solving the various puzzles he was considering, when he found to his surprise that he had come back to his original camp. He knew it was his because of the dull, unimaginative designs of the webs that stretched between the trees.

He compared them to the webs he had encountered, even to the ones he had created the day before, and felt a certain shame that he had ever thought so simple a pattern could attract any prey. Then, suddenly, his tongue picked up the sound and the vibrations of something thrashing desperately. He made a quick round of his webs and found a medium-sized reptile in one of them.

It was weak, as if it had been stranded there for a couple of days without food or water, as was probably the case. The thing that amazed Lennox was not that it was still alive, but that it had blundered into such a simplistic and unimaginative web in the first place.

Lennox put the reptile out of its misery with a quick, painless kill, then downed it voraciously. As he ate it, he considered this new information, which seemed to invalidate his prior conclusions: evidently a web *didn't* have to be as intricate as those he had seen. It could fulfill its purpose anyway, even when poorly conceived and crudely executed.

Then why waste time creating webs of greater complexity? Were they a form of art, which would imply sentience? Or did the Wheelers simply have an instinct to create intricate patterns? Or had Lennox just been lucky with this one web, and did the more complex webs tend to catch more prey?

He needed more information, and so he expanded his home territory by half, and on the new ground he created the most complicated webs he could spin, while leaving the old, simplistic webs where they were. Then he prepared himself for a couple of weeks of boredom while waiting for his unique database to supply him with some answers.

At the end of fifteen days, his primitive webs had captured eleven animals and avians, while his more sophisticated webs had captured five. Since the primitive webs covered twice the territory, the only conclusion he could draw was that the complexity of the webs had nothing to do with their efficiency at attracting and trapping prey animals.

The next thing to do was find out if the complexity was purposeful or instinctual.

He left his territory once more, and came upon another Wheeler about two hours later. It stopped its web-spinning and turned to him. There were no signs of aggression, so Lennox approached to within two feet of the Wheeler. It studied him carefully for a few moments, then went back to working on its web. Every few moments it would stop and turn to him again.

Is he inviting me to build my webs here? Or is he just wondering when I'm going to leave?

Lennox didn't know what was expected of him, but just on the chance that he *was* being invited to stay, he rolled over to a pair of nearby trees and made a crude rectangular web between them.

The Wheeler rolled over and seemed very agitated. It ripped Lennox's web apart and sprayed the beginnings of a new web between the trees.

Lennox examined the new web. It was circular, with eight spokes extending from a point in the middle.

So why are rectangles bad and circles good?

Lennox tore down the web and created his own circle. The Wheeler looked at it, and then at Lennox.

Okay, so it's not a great circle. It's a good enough one. It's round. What the hell do you want me to do next?

Puzzled, Lennox rolled back a few feet to give the Wheeler room to show him what he was doing right or wrong, but the Wheeler merely extended its tongue at him for another moment, and then returned to the web it had originally been working on.

Lennox followed it, stopping a few feet away, and observed until it was finished. Then it rolled to an old web, tore it down, and started creating a new one.

This doesn't make any sense. The webs hold their structural integrity for weeks, and they're as sticky now as when you created them. So why are you tearing this one apart and making a new one?

Suddenly his tongue sensed a creature in distress. The Wheeler raced off, and Lennox followed it at a safe distance. A large avian was stuck in a web, flapping its wings and screeching in terror. The Wheeler instantly killed it and began eating it. Lennox approached to within fifteen feet, and the Wheeler immediately made a mock charge, just enough of a show of aggression so that Lennox backed off.

He waited until the Wheeler was through eating. About a third of the avian was left, and as the Wheeler rolled off he tentatively approached the remains. The Wheeler stopped and watched him, but showed no sign that it intended to stop him, and he gratefully gobbled down the last of the prey.

He remained in the vicinity of the Wheeler for two more hours, but it paid him no further attention, and eventually he decided to return to his home territory.

He got there just before dark, to find that some other Wheeler had added a few designs to one of his webs. They were a series of interlinked triangles, and as he made the rounds of his webs, he found the same pattern had been added to each.

Did this mean someone had taken over his turf, and left him a message to that effect? He didn't know.

He spent the night by one of his webs, hoping that the intruding Wheeler would wait until morning to come by and that he would have thought of a response to it by then. But when morning came, he was still alone.

He was making the rounds of his webs when he sensed the vibrations of a small beast caught in one of them. He hurried to it—and found a Wheeler positioned between himself and the rodent that was struggling futilely to free itself.

They remained motionless for almost five minutes, facing each other. The Wheeler made no attempt to run him off, nor did it show any interest in killing and eating the rodent. Finally Lennox could stand the tension no longer, and rolled forward.

The Wheeler immediately rolled aside, giving Lennox a clear path to the web. It was one of his very first ones, just five lines strung across the gap between two trees, looking exactly like a line of sheet music with no notes on it.

Lennox killed the rodent, and as he began eating it, he became aware that the Wheeler had moved beside him, and was now creating the same pattern of triangles on his web that he had seen on his other webs. It made no attempt to take the remains of the rodent away from him, but backed away and watched him expectantly.

You know I'm not going to charge you, so what do you expect of me?

Just to see what would happen, Lennox wrapped his tongue around the uneaten portion of the rodent and tossed it over to the Wheeler, which consumed it with a single gulp.

Then the Wheeler approached him again, and created a series of interlinked diamonds on the web.

Why diamonds, when it was triangles before? It means something—but what?

And suddenly it dawned on him.

If it means anything at all, he's communicating with me! The message has changed from triangles to these linked diamonds. What could he possibly be saying to me now that he wasn't saying before?

Lennox stared at the diamonds, and then at the Wheeler, which was standing a couple of feet away, looking sated.

He's thanking me!

Lennox thought back to all the other webs he had found, to the intricate patterns that rarely repeated from one web to the next. He recalled the Wheeler he had met the day before tearing down his web because it made no sense, and then ignoring him when he didn't respond to the Wheeler's web.

Of course! I'm the illiterate village idiot. They try to talk to me, and when I can't respond, they just feel sorry for me and ignore me!

He turned to the web and created a meaningless pattern. This Wheeler responded just as the previous one had, by tearing it down and creating a new one—only this time Lennox paid close attention. He didn't know quite how to question the patterns, but as long as he shared his food, he felt confident that the Wheeler would stay around long enough to teach him. It would be a long, slow, laborious process, just like learning to speak a new language, but new languages were one of his specialties, and he had no doubt that eventually he could master it.

Eleven weeks later he bade his mentor good-bye and set out to communicate with the rest of the Wheelers. They had something the Republic wanted, and they would need an interpreter to make sure they got the best possible deal.

He stopped at the first web he came to and left a message on it:

Greetings. My name is Lennox. Bring all your brethren here tomorrow. We have important things to discuss.

He made the rounds of the neighboring territories, leaving similar messages, and was gratified to find a message waiting for him when he returned:

We will be there, Brother Lennox.

TWENTY-SIX

W hat have you done to him?'' demanded Angela Stone.

"Nothing that he didn't agree to," replied Nora Wallace.

"Why can't I see him?"

"He doesn't want to see you. I'm simply honoring his request."

"I want to hear it from him!"

"He is incapable of speech, Miss Stone," answered Nora.

"What?" said Angela, stunned.

"He has no vocal chords."

"But he *loves* to talk! I think he liked lecturing even more than writing. How could you take that away from him?"

"It was his decision," replied Nora. "He can no longer talk to you or to anyone else."

"I want to see him anyway."

"I don't think that would be wise."

"What do *you* know?" snapped Angela. "I'm not just his ex-wife. I'm his literary agent. I have professional reasons for meeting with him."

Nora Wallace sighed deeply. "If I took you to him, you would find a sluglike creature with no hands or feet, no eyes or ears or nostrils, a *thing* that sees and hears and communicates solely by manipulating a fifteen-inch tongue. It lives on live animals, and refuses dead ones. Its sole means of locomotion is to roll across the floor from one side of its empty chamber to the other." She paused. "Are you quite sure you want to see him?"

"Can something like that live?" asked Angela.

"Certainly. And under the right circumstances, on the right world, it can function better than you or I could." Nora looked at the distraught woman facing her. "I'll be blunt: there's nothing human left of Xavier Lennox, nothing that you could recognize as the man you once knew. He has no desire to see you or any other human being. His only wish is to be transformed once again."

"If he can't speak, how do you know that?"

"We've rigged a computer that he can manipulate with that remarkable tongue of his."

"And he *talks* to you like that?"

"His communications have been extremely limited. He reported on the success of his mission. Since then, his only messages have been a pair of brief sentences, endlessly repeated."

"And what are they?"

"The first is 'No visitors.' The second is 'Change me.' "

"Perhaps he wants you to change him back into a Man."

"I've asked a few times. His only answer is 'strait-jacket,' which I interpret to mean he considers wearing a Man's body to be the equivalent of wearing a strait-jacket."

"How many more surgeries can he take?"

"Probably one, possibly two. We simply don't know. He's a pathfinder; no one has ever undergone what he has. Except for his brain, heart, and lungs, there's not much of the original Xavier Lennox left unchanged."

"How can he live like that?"

"I'll be perfectly honest with you, Miss Stone. If we agree to change him again, this will be the last time. Each time he returns he is less and less willing to share his information with us. On his most recent assignment, he wound up negotiating *for* his new species and *against* the Republic. He is changing each time, not just physically, but psychologically as well. Oh, he finds ways to adapt to each world and to infiltrate each society, but I suspect that were he to be given a psychological test— we've tried, but he refuses to take it—he would be certifiable by human standards. Yet I also think that he is a perfectly sane specimen of a Wheeler. Each time he assimilates into an alien society, he loses more of his humanity. All that seems to remain is his desire to learn, and his ability to overcome whatever obstacles his new worlds throw at him."

"You've destroyed a brilliant human being," said

Angela bitterly. "If I thought I could get away with it, I'd charge you with murder."

"You'd never succeed," said Nora. "These have all been *his* decisions, not mine. Whatever he is, whatever he's becoming, it's a result of the choices he has made for himself."

"You could still change him back into Xavier Lennox."

Nora shook her head. "We could change him back into the physical representation of the Xavier Lennox you knew—although that would be illegal without his permission, and he'll never give it. But even if he did, he wouldn't be Xavier Lennox. He'd be something that thinks alien thoughts in alien languages, that has seen and done things that would drive most Men mad. Just the transformations themselves would be enough to turn a normal man into a raving psychotic. Think of it: to go under the knife as one thing, and to wake up minus some senses and organs and abilities you've had all your life, but also to have new ones that cannot even be described to someone who doesn't possess them." She paused. "Personally, I find it horrifying—but the man who used to be Xavier Lennox seems to find it addictive."

Angela Stone was silent for a very long moment. Finally she took a deep breath, exhaled, and looked at Nora Wallace.

"If he's an addict," she said, "you're the cause of it. What you did to him is no different from what a drug dealer does to schoolchildren. He was a productive human being—a damned important one—and you've turned him into some kind of alien thrill-seeker. How can you live with yourself?"

"As long as he can live with *him*self, I can live with myself," answered Angela bluntly. "I'm sure he has his own agenda, but it happens to coincide with the Republic's. He has saved three alien worlds from genocide."

"Really?"

"Really."

"An achievement like that, made at such personal cost, should be made known to everyone." She sighed. "He'll never write about it, will he?"

"No, he won't."

Angela walked to the door. "He loved music, you know. Will he ever be able to enjoy it again?"

"I don't know."

"And reading. The older and mustier the book, the more he loved it." She paused. "Has he read a book since you've known him?"

"No, I don't think so."

"He was a valuable human being before your department got hold of him."

"Believe it or not, I sympathize with your position, Miss Stone," said Nora seriously. "If you wish to talk again in the future . . ."

"No," said Angela. "There's nothing left to say."

She waited for the door to slide back, then turned to Nora one last time. "What is it that he wants?" she asked, her face a mask of confusion and despair.

"I really don't know," answered Nora truthfully. "I sometimes wonder if *he* knows any longer."

TWENTY-SEVEN

G ood afternoon, Xavier," said Nora Wallace, entering the empty chamber.

The Wheeler stared eyelessly at her, its tongue tasting her scent.

"Your former wife came here again this morning." Nora paused, watching for a reaction. "I told her that you didn't want to see her."

The Wheeler offered no response.

"Your computer is right there. Is there anything you'd like me to say to her?"

The Wheeler remained impassive.

"Is there anything you'd like to say to *me*?"

The Wheeler's tongue darted out to the computer.

CHANGE ME.

"I know, I know," said Nora. "We're waiting for

Doctor Ngoni and her staff to determine whether we *can* change you into what we need.''

CHANGE ME, repeated the Wheeler.

Suddenly a new question occurred to Nora. ''Are you in any pain as a Wheeler? Is that why you're in such a hurry to undergo another series of operations?''

NO. CHANGE ME.

''I told you: we're exploring possibilities.''

She put a reassuring hand atop the Wheeler. It darted across the room so quickly that it startled her.

''Did I hurt you?'' she asked.

The Wheeler rolled back to the computer.

DON'T TOUCH ME AGAIN.

''I didn't mean to hurt you.''

NO PAIN. JUST REPUGNANCE.

''Repugnance?'' she repeated. ''But I'm your own species, Xavier.''

NO LONGER.

''Would you find tactile contact by a Firefly or a Hawkhorn repugnant?'' asked Nora.

No response.

''You're not answering the question.''

CHANGE ME.

''This is becoming a very one-sided conversation. If you type Change Me one more time, I shall leave.''

BIG FUCKING DEAL.

She grinned in spite of herself. At least the Lennox she knew hadn't totally vanished. And as long as he had reappeared, she decided to try to draw him out.

''Have you given any thought to what you want to do after this next transformation?''

The Wheeler gave no indication that it had heard her, and she asked the question again.

CHANGE ME.

"We *are* changing you, damn it!" she snapped irritably. "Does nothing else in the universe interest you?"

CHANGE ME.

"I'm losing my patience with you, Xavier!"

CHANGE ME CHANGE ME CHANGE ME

TWENTY-EIGHT

And change him they did. Where once he had long, muscular arms, now he had webbed extensions with huge membranes attached to them. He couldn't fly, of course; but he *could* glide.

He found that he also had the ability to consciously alter his metabolism. His training was simple enough: he was placed in rooms of varying temperatures without any protective covering, and within seconds he had totally adjusted to them. The same held true for foods: he was given alien animals cooked and uncooked, alien grain, and noxious fluids that would have killed the original Xavier William Lennox. He consumed them all without any discomfort or adverse side effects.

His voice was back, but it could only form delicate tinkling, chiming sounds, like crystal upon fine crystal. He was unable to articulate any words, but it was thought that his new species communicated by melody and inflection, and for that reason the colonists had dubbed them Singers.

He had eyes once again—huge, multifaceted things, capable of seeing in almost total darkness. His ears were large, and able to differentiate the sound of one violin in an array of fifty strings playing the same melody.

His face looked not unlike a giant insect's, but his body resembled nothing more than a glowing silver bullet. His hands—claws, actually—grew out of the ends of his wing membranes. His legs—there were three of them—weren't much good for running, but once he planted them, nothing less than a hurricane could make him move against his will. Finally, there were small suction cups in the palms of his hands and the soles of his feet, with which he could scale the sheerest of walls, or pause at any height and in any position with no danger of falling to the ground.

His assignment this time was simple and straightforward. The nine hundred human colonists on Monticello IV had come down with a wasting disease, a virus carried by the microscopic snail-like flukes that lived and bred in their water supply. They found a way to treat the water, but by then the entire colony was infected. It was a disease that was very slow to manifest itself, much like AIDS had been on Earth two millennia earlier, but, untreated, it was every bit as fatal.

Then, just when it seemed that there was no cure for it, the medics who had been assigned to the Monticello colony found out that the Singers, the only sentient local life-form, carried a microbe in their blood that actually killed the virus. A quart of Singer blood would supply just enough of the microbes to cure a single human.

Because the disease was slow-acting and the Republic was painfully aware of its image as an aggressor, Lennox had been given three months to land on Monticello IV, make contact with the Singers, and convince them to donate enough blood to eradicate the disease. If they did not agree by then, the navy would show up and forcibly take it by the gallon, doubtless spilling far more than it needed.

Lennox had argued that three months wasn't enough time, that it might take him that long just to learn the rudiments of the language, but it was all the Department of Alien Affairs was willing to grant him. He could agree to their terms and become a Singer, he could remain a Wheeler, or he could revert to human form. There was no fourth alternative.

Given the choices, his decision surprised no one.

TWENTY-NINE

At first glance, it appeared that the majority of the Singers lived in lush green valleys. Now and then they would stray too close to the passes leading to adjoining valleys, which were also populated by Singers, and a guard would swoop down from atop a hill, gliding gracefully on the thermals, and warn them back in its melodic, chiming voice.

At least, that was Lennox's conclusion after viewing them from high overhead. Then the Republic ship set him down a couple of miles away from the first of the interconnected valleys. He took a deep breath of the fresh, clean air—and his nostrils were assailed by an unfamiliar scent, one so sweet and intoxicating that he actually began salivating. He followed it and soon came to the valley. There were perhaps fifty inhabitants in it, and now he knew what had drawn him here. They were all females, and some of them were in estrus.

He had taken less than a dozen steps into the valley when he heard a loud, harsh melody overhead. He looked up and saw a Singer swooping down toward him, claws extended, jaws open.

He spun aside at the last minute, and as the Singer spread his wings and gained height, Lennox began running as best he could on his three legs, keeping to the valley wall. The Singer made three more attempts to reach him, and then he was in the protected pass between the first and second valley.

Gasping for breath, Lennox stood perfectly still and tried to analyze what had happened. He had walked into a valley filled with females, and an instant later a male had attacked him. Why? Was the Singer protecting his territory or his harem? Or both?

The pass between the valleys was about seventy yards long, and Lennox walked to the end of it. The second valley also held a number of females, and as he looked up, he saw two males gliding on the winds, headed for each other intent on combat. They met with a tremendous *thud*! about sixty feet above the valley floor, and the smaller of the two instantly plummeted down toward the ground. He managed to spread his wings just before he hit, and arched upward with the larger male in hot pursuit. He couldn't find a thermal strong enough to lift him over the top of the valley, and he landed about two-thirds of the way up the wall. The larger male tore into him with claw and tooth, and he fought a defensive fight, backing up the hill foot by foot. When he reached the top, he plunged over the edge and out of Lennox's field of vision.

Lennox spent the rest of the day hidden in the pass, watching first one valley and then the other, as the two dominant Singer males kept chasing off other males who seemed compelled to challenge them every few hours.

Finally, just after dawn the next morning, another male entered the second valley from the one beyond it. But unlike those that had flown in and challenged the Singer who ruled from atop the valley wall, this one walked across the floor, stooped over, its claws clasped together above its head, its wings hanging limp and useless. The Singer looked down once, then paid the newcomer no further attention as it stopped at a stream, slaked its thirst, and then proceeded to the pass where Lennox was hiding.

The moment it left the valley it unclasped its claws and began walking erect. It came to a stop when it saw Lennox, and began speaking to him in its singsong, chiming voice. Lennox tried to answer back by repeating the sounds, but he could not make himself understood, and finally he just stopped speaking and stared at the Singer, waiting to see what it would do next.

It chimed one last melody at him, then walked past and stepped into the first valley, once again stooping over and clasping its claws above its head. It was a subservient posture if Lennox had ever seen one, and he decided to imitate it, stepping out a few feet behind the Singer. He never looked up as they crossed the valley, but the Singer above him made no attempt to harm him this time, and they passed through unmolested.

The Singer he had been following turned and chimed to him again. Lennox made no reply, but indicated through such signs as he could make with his limited arm and hand movement that he wished to come along. The Singer chimed again and started walking off, and Lennox fell into step behind him.

They walked for almost five miles until they came to what seemed to be the same river that ran through the valleys. There were hundreds of males camped by the riverbank, and Lennox noticed that almost all of them were either very young or very old. Those few who weren't bore the marks of recent injuries.

Most of them were scavenging for fish and insects, and Lennox joined them. He knew that his body was omnivorous, and he could just as easily have plucked some fruits from the nearby trees—but he also sensed that he required protein, and could get it in much greater quantity from animal life.

The other Singers were using crude nets to catch their fish, but Lennox had no desire to spend a day or more weaving a net, so he waded out into the water, hunched over, and spread his wings just above the surface. The fish, seeking to get out of that section of the water that had been warmed by the sun, sought out the artificial shade Lennox had created. He allowed his fingers to dip very gently into the water, and when a fish swam through, he closed them, grabbed it, and quickly tossed it onto the shore. By the time he had repeated the process twice more, a number of the Singers came by to watch with open curiosity.

After tossing his sixth fish onto the shore, Lennox straightened up and left the river. He gave one fish to his traveling companion and tossed four of them to a quartet of withered old Singers who looked like they had been a long time between meals. The old Singers snatched the fish up and raced off with them, but the Singer who had led Lennox to the river sat down next to him and began eating.

Lennox held his own fish up questioningly, the Singer said something, Lennox repeated it, the Singer corrected his pronunciation, and Lennox's linguistic education began in earnest. By nightfall he had learned two dozen words, and he felt confident that within a week, possibly even less, he would be able to make his most basic wants known. After that, like all languages, it was just a matter of repetition and diligence.

During the course of the day, when he was not learning new words, he was analyzing what he had seen thus far, and coming to some tentative conclusions. The basic social order here resembled that of many herd animals he had seen on Earth and elsewhere. The dominant males claimed their territories—in this case, the valleys—and tried to keep any female who wandered in from wandering out again. A few pretenders to the thrones tried to defeat them in battle and take away their harems. The rest of the males, those too young, too old, or too weak to fight, lived in bachelor colonies on the outskirts. Some were preparing for the day when they would attempt to unseat the dominant males and win their harems; some were dreaming of the days, long past, when they, too, had been the possessors of harems; and some, Lennox was sure, were simply nursing their wounds and counting the days before they could make another attempt to defeat the Singers who patrolled their territories from atop the valley walls.

He had been attacked when he initially entered the first valley because he had walked erect, doubtless a threatening posture in the eyes of the dominant Singer. When he had stooped over and locked his hands over his head, he was telling the Singer that he simply wanted passage through the valley and that he had no intention of trying to make off with any of the harem . . . and since even the dominant Singers could be worn down by endless fights to prove their supremacy, they were more than happy to give those males that displayed proper subservience free passage through their domains.

Lennox lingered by the river with the bachelors for the better part of two months. Every day a few would go off to test their mettle against the dominant Singers. Most of the time they would come back a few hours later, figuratively licking their wounds. Once in a while they wouldn't return at all. And on very rare occasions, a defeated Singer who had just lost his harem would join the group, torn and bleeding and filled with rage—or occasionally so badly beaten that all hatred and bitterness had been replaced by an all-encompassing self-pity.

Finally Lennox felt he had enough of a grasp of the language that he could address the bachelors. He gathered a few hundred of them around him and explained that the Men who had settled on Monticello IV had come down with a fatal disease, and that the only way to cure it would be with the donated blood of perhaps a thousand Singers. He asked for volunteers, both to give blood and to pass the word to other bachelor colonies.

It went over like a lead balloon.

They couldn't see any reason to give blood or anything else to aliens who had come, uninvited, to live on *their* world. Besides, their only contact with Man had occurred when Man had captured and killed four of their number in order to dissect them and learn the secret of their immunity. Man was not their favorite species, and as far as they were concerned, the sooner the last Man was dead, the better.

Lennox didn't argue with them. In fact, he found himself agreeing with everything they said. But he planned to present Nora Wallace with his own demands when this assignment was over, and he knew he had more chance of getting what he wanted if his mission was successful. Besides, if he failed, he was condemning thousands of Singers to death, and he *was* a Singer.

So he began exploring alternatives, and finally he hit upon the one that seemed the likeliest to provide a solution to his problem.

He scoured the riverbed for sharp stones, found a few to his liking, and left the colony for three days, going into a nearby forest. He spent the time finding branches of the proper shape and strength and then working on them with his stones until he had carved some thirty short, thick spears. He carried them back to the bachelor camp, laid them in a neat pile, and once again summoned his companions.

"If I show you how to defeat the Tall Ones"—their term for the dominant Singers—"how many of you will allow the Men to take a small amount of blood from each member of the harem that you control?"

"We cannot defeat them," complained a Singer.

"That is why we are here and they are there. They are stronger."

"I will prove to you that you can overcome their strength."

"How?"

"I will defeat the first Tall One myself," said Lennox. "But only those who pledge me the blood of their harems may watch and learn."

Most of them were dubious, but seven Singers, dreams of sex and glory dancing before their multifaceted eyes, agreed to Lennox's terms. He had hoped for more, but seven was a start, and once they succeeded, he was sure that others would follow.

He pulled eight spears out of the pile and cradled them in his arms, then marched off toward the valleys, followed by his seven volunteers. When they reached the first valley, he instructed the Singers to take their subservient posture, enter the valley, and watch what happened next.

They all agreed, but none of them moved out.

"What is the problem?" demanded Lennox. "I told you to go into the valley."

"It will take you almost an hour to climb to the top of the hill and attack the Tall One," answered a Singer. "We will wait until you are halfway up before entering. That way we will not seem to be lingering too long."

"Go now," said Lennox. "This will be over in less than a minute."

"You cannot possibly climb that fast."

"I don't plan to climb at all."

"You give up the advantage of flight and still expect to win?" replied the Singer. "It cannot be done!"

"It has not been done *yet,*" corrected Lennox. "Now enter the valley."

The seven Singers looked at him as if he were mad, but they did as he ordered, stooping over and clasping their hands above their heads.

Lennox laid the spears down in a neat pile, then selected the strongest of them, and walked, erect, into the valley.

A moment later he heard the furious chiming of a Tall One, and looked up to see it swooping down upon him, claws extended, teeth bared. He waited patiently until it was almost upon him, then braced the shaft of the spear against the ground and crouched down until the point was perhaps a foot above his head. The Tall One, which had never seen a weapon before, continued his attack, and impaled himself on the spear as he tried to reach Lennox, who calmly stepped aside and watched the Singer's death throes.

A moment later the seven male Singers walked over cautiously and stared in awe at the dead Tall One.

"You see?" said Lennox. "If you will do as I did, you will each have your harem before the day is over."

"You killed a Tall One, and there is not a mark on your body!" exclaimed one of them.

"You did not even meet him on the winds!" said another.

"It wasn't necessary," answered Lennox. He then proceeded to explain and demonstrate the use of his weapon, and he passed a spear to each of them.

By nightfall there were seven new Tall Ones, and when word reached the bachelor colony, Lennox had more volunteers than he could possibly use. Within a week there had been a total turnover of Tall Ones, and Lennox sent word to the Republic's medical team that he had lined up more than twelve hundred blood donors for them.

Then it was time for his final confrontation with Nora Wallace.

THIRTY

Lennox was working at the computer when Nora Wallace entered his room. He was still a Singer, and there was no furniture that could accommodate him, so he had simply attached his feet to a wall with their suction cups and was now hanging straight out, parallel with the floor, his insect's eyes inches from the holographic screen.

When his visitor appeared he detached himself from the wall and stood before her, trying to hide the repugnance he felt in her presence, just as she tried to hide her revulsion at his appearance.

"Good morning, Mister Lennox," she said.

His answer was unintelligible to her.

"I've just come back from the Department's headquarters on Deluros VIII," she continued. "Our budget has been cut—well, redirected, actually—and your particular project has lost its funding.'' She paused, trying to discern a reaction, but finding none. ''It makes very little difference anyway. As I told you after your last surgery, it is the opinion of Doctor Ngoni's staff that you can only survive one more transformation.''

Lennox merely stared at her, as if waiting for her to continue.

''In appreciation for your unique services to the Republic, they have set aside enough money to pay for that transformation, but since we have no assignment for you, you are free to choose any race you want—or to go back to being a Man.''

Lennox stepped forward and wrote his answer on the computer.

NEVER.

''I thought not,'' said Nora.

He wrote another message.

''This doesn't make any sense, Mister Lennox,'' she said. ''It's all garbled. Part of it looks like some intricate design, and over here you've written what seems to be some musical notes.''

MY MISTAKE. IT'S GETTING MORE DIFFICULT ALL THE TIME TO THINK IN TERRAN.

''What languages are those?''

UNIMPORTANT. He paused, trying to order his thoughts and translate them into terms she could understand. I HAVE BEEN THINKING ABOUT THE NEXT TRANSFORMATION.

''Doctor Ngoni says you can choose any oxygen-breathing race except for the Domarians and the Mollutei.''

I KNOW WHAT I WANT.

"Good. What is it?"

WATCH.

He entered a number of commands, and the machine slowly pieced together a holograph in response to them.

"I've never seen such a thing before," said Nora, studying the image. "It's quite beautiful." She stared at it intently. "One might almost say awesome. What planet does it live on?"

NONE. Then he added: YET.

"Is it your own creation?" she asked, surprised that she wasn't more surprised.

YOUR CREATION. MY DESIGN.

"You'll have to consult with Doctor Ngoni," said Nora. "Anything's possible, I suppose—but why did you create *this* particular design?"

I LIKE IT.

"That's no reason to spend the rest of your life as a . . . a whatever-it-is."

WHAT BETTER REASON IS THERE?

Nora considered the question, realized she didn't have an answer, and finally shrugged.

"What will you do once you have taken this shape?"

I HAVE MY WORK.

"I told you: we've lost our funding."

MY WORK, NOT YOURS.

"Would you care to tell me what this work entails?" asked Nora.

NO, I WOULD NOT.

"Or where you plan to do it?"

ON A WORLD WHERE I FIT.

She stared at the hologram again. "There has never been a world where this could fit."

THEN FIND ONE.

"I'll do my best. We owe you that much."

YES, YOU DO.

Nora had the machine present her with a series of hard copies of Lennox's creation, showing it from all possible angles.

"I'll drop this off with Doctor Ngoni," she said. "I'm sure she'll want to discuss the details with you." Nora walked to the door, then hesitated and looked back. "This may be the last time I see you. I've been transferred to the Albion Cluster."

The thing that was no longer Xavier William Lennox was lost in its own thoughts and did not answer. She stared at it for a long moment, then walked out of the room without telling it that she was both proud and ashamed of the part she had played in the strange trajectory of its life.

THIRTY-ONE

The sole inhabitant of Alpha Bengston II, since renamed Xavier, stood on the ground and watched the ship that had brought him vanish into the stratosphere on its way back to the worlds of the Republic.

It was an impressive creature. It had the multifaceted eyes of a Singer, combined with the night vision of a Firefly. A single ridged horn, possessing all the properties of the Hawkhorns' Horn of Perception, rose from its forehead. The tongue of a Wheeler shot out of its mouth, testing the breeze for odors and signs of movement.

From its back sprung two large wings, Singer wings that could glide on the high thermals. Its body was covered with feathers, not the yellow-orange-and-blue pattern of the *droika*, but a brilliant, glowing, multihued pattern borrowed from the webs of the Wheelers. Its powerful, muscular arms terminated in sturdy hands that possessed two opposing thumbs each. Its three legs, slender but powerful, ended in the circular feet of the Hawkhorns, feet that expanded upon contact with the ground but contracted when it lifted them.

As it listened to the contented sounds of the vegetation surrounding it, it tried out some of the other features of its new body: the telescoping arms and legs, the multiple voices ranging from delicate chiming to bone-jarring roars. The gills would have to wait until it came upon a lake or a river, and the infrared vision until the darkness came.

It surveyed its surroundings. Off to the west was a mountain range, and its long, agile tongue picked up the scent of water from the north. There were forests and valleys, savannahs and deserts, all to be explored. And there were birds and animals and fish, none of them ever seen before, all to be studied, as well as captured and eaten.

The creature searched its mind, trying to find some regret at never seeing a human being again, but could find none. They had served their purpose, and now it was time to serve its own. It unpacked the computer and the generator, the only two things it had brought along to this new world, and set up a workstation.

The months and years ahead would be busy. There was a Firefly bible to translate, an incredibly complex Wheeler language to codify, a symphony of Singer philosophy to compose, a Hawkhorn history to write. There was a new body to learn. And there were other things—strange thoughts and alien images—to interpret before its time ran out.

Time was the enemy. There was so much to do, so

many things to sort out. Perhaps someday, if it lived long enough, it might even listen to the tiny remnant of Xavier William Lennox that lay buried deep within it and try to regain contact with its long-departed humanity.

But the remnant grew smaller with each passing day, and somehow it knew that it would vanish forever before that eventuality came to pass.

THE BEST OF SF FROM TOR

THE BEST OF SF FROM TOR